Tales from the Night Rainbow
Mo'olelo o na Pō Mākole

The Story of a Woman, a People, and an Island

An oral history as told by
Kaili'ohe Kame'ekua
of Kamalo, Moloka'i
1816–1931

"In Loving Memory of Pali Jae Lee and Koko Willis"

Family Edition – 1986
Second Printing – 1987
Third Printing – 1988
Fourth Printing – 1990
Fifth Printing – 1994
Sixth Printing – 2001
Seventh Printing – 2005
Eighth Printing – 2010

ISBN 0-9628030-0-6
Printed in the United States

Cover design by Hans Loffel with a drawing by James Stickney
'Ohe kapala design by Philip Markwart

This book
is written in first
person. The stories are
being shared with us by our
big grandma, Kaili'ohe Kame'ekua
of Kamalo, Moloka'i.   1816-1931.

There are many kinds of rainbows. The night too has rainbows. One, the encircling ring around the moon, is only a weather sign. The other night rainbow, *Na Po Mokole,* is seen only by a few. It is the Spirit rainbow. The rainbow that holds our ancestors. When it is seen it is a great blessing from all our family who have gone out of flesh. Many healings take place at this time, for our spirit family knows our needs and tries to help us. They give us knowledge and rekindle the light when it is weak. It is a time of unity, a time for family—a reawakening or renewal for those in body. There is no greater blessing on earth than the blessing of the Night Rainbow.

Ho'ola'a
DEDICATION

'Āmama, Ua Noa, Lele Wale
The Kapu is Finished, the Words Fly Free

To Kaili'ohe Kame'ekua:
Kumu, Ku'u Hoa, Kupuna

To Kāmauliauhonua o Moloka'i
Kona Akua, Kona 'Āumakua Uhi, 'Āina Pua

To the Light Carriers, acknowledged and unacknowledged:
Malcolm Chun, Sam Ka'ai, Aina Keawe, Earl Neller, Karen and Ray Lovell,
Mui Lang and Franklin Baker, Bee Olson, Lele Wahine Gulden, Malia and
Kawika McClelland, all our children and to all the nameless people who have
shed their Light to make the world a better place.

Me Ke Aloha Nui

Papa Kuhikuhi
TABLE OF CONTENTS

Mahalo
'Ōlelo Ho'omaika'i
ACKNOWLEDGEMENTS

To Karen Lovell who helped in all areas of this edition; to Teddy Mahi'ai who helped us find many of our family sites and gave constant support; to Malia McClelland: artist, daughter and friend, whose artwork enhances the family story; to the staffs of the Children's Mission Society Library and the Hawaiian Historical Society for assistance in verification of dates and data whenever it was possible.

Me Ke Aloha Nui

'Ōlelo-ha'i-mua

FOREWORD

This book began as a compilation of stories and remembrances for the children of the 'Ohana Kame'ekua. The family elders wanted the children to know who they were and the history of their family.

In 1983 the elders of the family decided to share these stories with other families of Moloka'i and Hawaii Nei, so they too could know something of their past. Historians and anthropologists differ with some of the material but this is how the stories were told and this is how they are presented.

Kauakokoula Kuhaimoana Kaimana Willis
Theodore Keli'ikahi Mahi'ai
Joseph Umioliloapuakalehua Nakagawa
Gregory Kamehameha ai-lu'au Keliinui

Ruling Elders: 'Ohana Kame'ekua

MAJESTIC HALAWA

THEODORE MAHI‘AI AND
JOHN KOKO WILLIS

JOSEPH NAKAGAWA

GREGORY KELIINUI

‘Ohana Kame‘ekua

RULING ELDERS

Ho'ohui
INTRODUCTION

Our family elders have agreed that the truths held "in" family should be shared with all the children of our *'ohana* (family) and the children of other clans who have lost their family stories.

History changes with the years and the view of the person telling the story. How one "thinks" an event occurred is often construed as history. In fact, most of these accounts are not accurate at all.

We can only speculate on how errors began. Any story told and retold will change unless every small detail is learned and repeated with an accuracy that is true to each breath and pause. There is another reason for change. For that, our own people carry the shame. Hawaiians have long held the idea that the *ha'ole* (foreigner) would believe anything he is told (since he views the Hawaiian as savage—make the most of it—scare him a little). It was a way of "paying back" for the lost Hawaiian gods, laws, and land; but most of all, the loss of Hawaiian humanity.

The outlandish stories have come back to roost, for now many of Hawai'i's own children believe our people roasted and ate Captain Cook and other similar made-up stories. It can no longer be viewed as a joke. Hawaiian history has become mostly fiction. How do we then correct these errors? How do we give our children pride in their heritage when there is no one to tell them?

Our family was blessed for we had big grandma Kaili'ohe. Although she taught us to not tell stories "out-of-family," to listen to the boasters and the braggers, and to keep our truths to ourselves, she saw it as very important for our own children to know the truth about who and what they were.

Of Kaili'ohe's children, only two daughters expressed interest in perpetuating the family history. The stories were learned and kept by them and a few of their children. Today, these few are quickly leaving us. Since we began this work most of the elders who shared their knowledge have joined their ancestors. It is important that these stories be in print so the children not yet born and those now growing can share in Kaili'ohe's knowledge.

Kaili'ohe was 17 when the missionaries came to Moloka'i. She was quite taken with their Bible for it held all the stories, all the genealogy, and it could be passed on and on without worry on anyone's part that it would change. Her dream envisioned a book like that for the Hawaiian people.

There have been many Hawaiian histories written. Most of them by foreigners. The few histories written by Hawaiians were written in Hawaiian. The foreigners who translated them into English took many liberties. This can be seen by comparing David Malo's original text of HAWAIIAN ANTIQUITIES which is again available in Hawaiian, and the translation by N.B. Emerson, 1898. Some things were told correctly, but most were changed by the translator to a biased Christian viewpoint.

This history is the story of the Kai-akea family of the *Mo'o* Clan, which traces its lineage back to at least 800 B.C. (if you use 4 generations to a century). Kaili'ohe was the granddaughter of Kai-akea, and the one chosen to learn the genealogy and historical chants of the family. She was born in 1816 (during the reign of Kamehameha I) and *hanai* (adopted) to Maka-weliweli to be taught these things. She was taught well. When still a child, she mastered the fun chants (like Paul Bunyan stories) of the family, then the history chants, and finally began work on the genealogy chants. She continued to learn until the death of her beloved *hanai* mother and teacher in 1840.

The Christian missionaries came to Moloka'i in 1832. Kaili'ohe saw nothing wrong in helping them build their *pili* grass church at Kalua'aha, or later a coral church; nor did she see anything wrong in helping gather workers to build the churches Father Damien wanted when he came to Moloka'i. She saw much that was good in what the foreigners brought. She was also wise enough to know that her own heritage must be preserved. When Judge Abe Fornander was working on his Hawaiian histories, he sent David Malo and others to Kaili'ohe for assistance, and finally went himself. Kaili'ohe had learned already to be cautious and she shared little.

Since she was born during the time of Kamehameha's unification of the islands and lived through the entire Monarchy period, she knew much of the history. She saw the islands overthrown by greedy foreigners, and witnessed the establishment of their Provisional Government. She died well after the islands became a territory of the United States. This history is as she, and other members of her family, told it. It is of a Hawai'i that few people can now believe existed. A mystical, magical place where love ruled and all men lived as brothers.

Recorded by her *mo'opuna kuakahi,* Pali and Koko

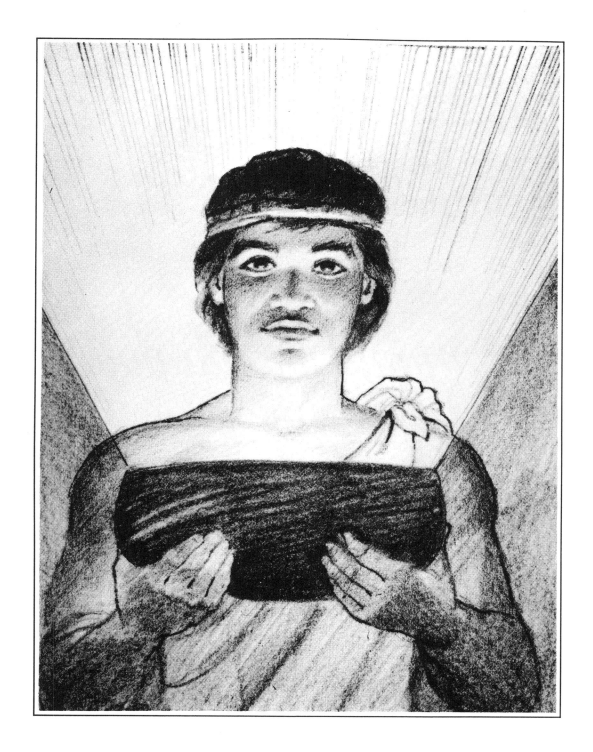

Ka Poʻe Kahiko

KAILIʻOHE'S STORIES OF THE ANCIENT PEOPLE

Ka Poʻe Kahiko

KAILIʻOHE'S STORIES OF THE ANCIENT PEOPLE

History, as anything else, is seen and understood by where a person stands on the mountain.

All people climb the same mountain. The mountain, however, has many pathways—each with a different view. A person knows and understands only what he sees from his own pathway, and as he moves, his view will change. Only when he reaches the top of the mountain will he see and understand all the views of mankind. But who among us has reached the top of the mountain? Tomorrow, we too will see a different view. We have not finished growing.

Most Hawaiian histories have been written from the pathways taken by foreigners who wrote Hawaiian history as they saw and believed things to be. It was not a Hawaiian view, or from a Hawaiian pathway. These stories I tell you are from a pathway taken by my family, on Molokaʻi. They are the stories as told by Kai-akea to my teacher and beloved mother Kaʻa kau Makaweliweli (whom I will refer to only as Makaweliweli) and she in turn taught to those of us who were part of her *halau* (school) in Kapualei.

The ancient ones were the people who were *maoli* (native) to Hawaii. Seven or eight hundred years ago the Tahitians came to our islands, and since then the stories of our origins and life have been dominated by their outlook. In many ways the Tahitians were a people similar to us, but in other ways we were as light is to the dark. The early ones lived with an attitude about life that gave them what we would call great *mana* (power) over their surroundings, but it is really the power of love and kinship working through the feelings of the objects we live among.

Our ancestors lived in small family communities and were guided by the elders of the family. The families were called *ʻohana,* and all of the families on the islands who were of our line were *ʻohana laha.* Today we would call that a clan. There were many clans in those days and many people. Different communities belonging to a clan wore *kapa* (clothing) of the same color, but they had different markings on their *kapa,* to show which part of

17

the clan they belonged. When someone met a stranger and he wore the family color, he could tell to which branch of the family he belonged by these differences.

Each family had what we call an *'aumakua,* a spirit felt as a living part of the family—a presence—like our ancestors, aware of us and ready at all times to show us the turns in our pathways. This spirit could be a part of anything or everything. Our family was a *mo'o* family. A *mo'o* is a giant lizard or dragon, however, we were kind to all creatures for they were our brothers. We felt more for the lizard because it was our belief that they brought us luck, protected us and watched over us.

Our family wore our hair shoulder length and the men wore short beards. Some other branches of the family cut their hair short and plucked their beards. All the descendents of Kanehoalani (the Kaiakea family) wore finger tattoos to show that we followed a holy life. Other branches of the family had other tattoos, and some wore no tattoos at all.

There were many clans in ancient days, each with its own color and its own *'aumakua.* There was the shark family with its colors of grey. There was the shell clan who wore a dark red, and the owl family who wore *kapa* of browns. The thunder clan of Maui wore only the darkest black. On O'ahu there were families who wore orange (Leeward families) and in Koolauloa there were families with beautiful pink *kapa.* There were three very different and beautiful red *kapa:* the Kanekapa, Ke kupa ohi and Ke akua lahu.

On Moloka'i the gods were Ku and Hina. The temples *(heiau)* had an upright stone for KU (the male god) and prostrate flat stone for HINA (the female god). The temples of our family had a light which burned at all times and someone was always there to tend to it.

It was the belief of our family line that we had been here from the beginning. People had gone out from our land to the East and to the West, and populated other lands. We had chants that told of such migrations from our islands.

We taught by stories and parables. One of the earliest and most important to us was:

> "Each child born has at birth, a Bowl of perfect Light. If he tends his Light it will grow in strength and he can do all things—swim with the shark, fly with the birds, know and understand all things. If, however, he becomes envious or jealous he drops a stone into his

Bowl of Light and some of the
Light goes out. Light and the
stone cannot hold the same
space. If he continues to put
stones in the Bowl of Light, the
Light will go out and he will become a stone. A stone does not
grow, nor does it move. If at
any time he tires of being a
stone, all he needs to do is turn the bowl upside down and the stones
will fall away and the Light will grow once more."

The stories or parables were teachings and reminders. The *maoli* had
stories of vines, trees, seeds, fish, earth, sea and sky: the things that were
common to the people and that they understood. When a child began to
speak, the family began to teach him about the world of which he was a
part.

> *Aloha* is being a part of all
> and all being a part of me.
> When there is pain—it is my pain.
> When there is joy—it is mine also.
> I respect all that is
> as part of the Creator and part of me.
> I will not willfully harm anyone or anything.
> When food is needed I will take only my need
> and explain why it is being taken.
> The earth, the sky, the sea are mine
> To care for, to cherish and to protect.
> This is Hawaiian—This is *Aloha!*

The ancient ones believed that all time is now and that we are each crea-
tors of our life's conditions. We create ourselves and everything that be-
comes a part of our lives. Any situation in which we might find ourselves is
brought about by learning the many pathways of life. When we wish to
change our circumstances, all we have to do is release our present condition. It will be gone. On the other hand, if we find it useful to continue, we
can hang on to the problem and not let it go.

The early ones believed that there was one body of life to which we
belonged. We had land, sea and sky. They, too, were a part of us. Everything that grew on our land and swam in our ocean we called brother and

sister. We were a part of all things and all things were a part of us. The old ones knew this and lived accordingly. They did not destroy. They spoke to a plant that was to be picked and explained why it was being done. A rock, before being used as a part of a new house platform or *heiau,* would be asked if it approved of being used in such a manner. If signs were against such use, the people needing the rock moved to another location and asked a different rock. It was far better to do something correctly than in a hurry or without regard for the effects of our actions.

We were taught that when the *mana* (personal power) is strong and people accept themselves as the powerful beings that they are—all things are possible. Moving rocks, for instance, need not be as big a burden if the rocks wish to be a part of the project. Men would carry the stone but need not carry the weight of the stone.

Such learning applied to all parts of life, especially in fishing and collecting food. When the needed amount was clearly understood, it became available. There was no want. There was no waste.

The early ones taught that there is no dividing line between two people. You cannot hit your brother without hitting yourself, your father and your mother. It is best, then, to hit no one. The early ones had no kings, no great war lords, no armies, no system of laws.

Around 1250 A.D., a priest named Pa'ao came on a visit from Tahiti. We knew Tahitians for there were many Tahitians who had come here to live. Any family who wished to come and live on these shores was welcomed and they were helped to establish themselves. They usually adapted to our way of life quickly and there was harmony among the families. All these people were considered to be Hawaiian. Where they came from was of no importance. The heart *(kana'au)* was what we saw and heard.

Pa'ao was noticed for many reasons. He came wearing white. The color was not used by us for it represented the absence of life. The men who came with him wore the Tahitian red *malo* (clothing) with which we were familiar. Pa'ao visited every island asking questions, always asking questions. People wanted to be helpful and so told him of harbors and tides, fertile valleys and all the things he asked about. No one thought much about it— he'd ask questions, the people tried to answer. Then suddenly he was gone. The people questioned each other about him. He made many feel an unease that they were not used to. They called him the man who wore death, because of his undyed *kapa.*

Several years later, we learned that Pa'ao did indeed wear death for he returned bringing devastation to our land.

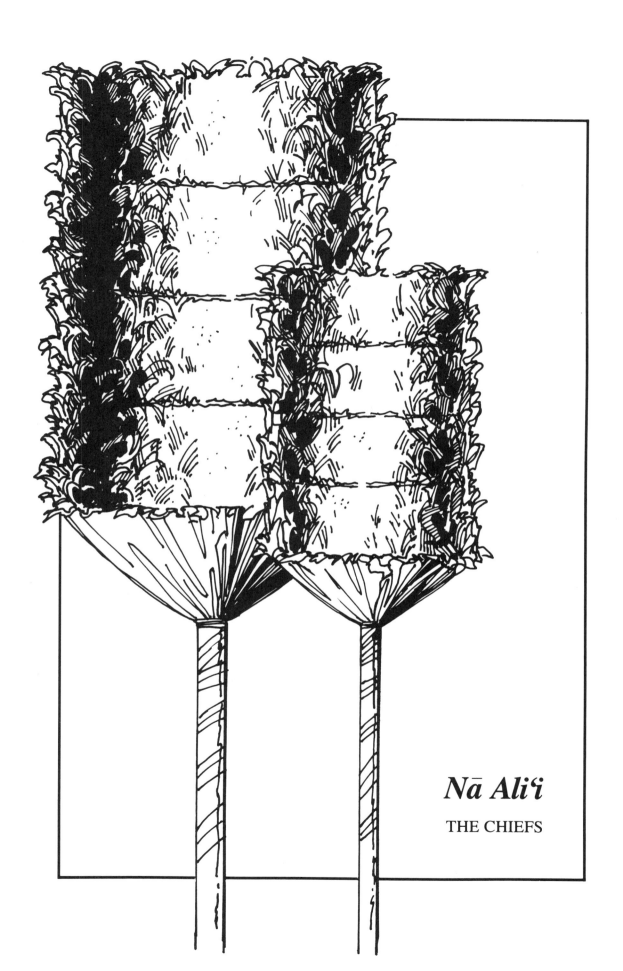

Nā Aliʻi

THE CHIEFS

Nā Aliʻi

THE CHIEFS

To us, they were invaders. Paʻao had gone back to Tahiti and gathered thousands of people to come to Hawaiʻi and take over the land. The men were tall fierce warriors. They did not believe in the force of light, only in the force of the closed fist, in mighty armies that killed, took and plundered.

The people on Lanaʻi were the first to see them approaching. They said the red *malo* of the invaders could be seen from horizon to horizon making the sea itself take on a red hue. Soon the sea did turn red with the blood of our people as thousands were slaughtered and enslaved. The native population that could, made a run for Kauaʻi where they would be safe. You had to be well schooled in the tides of Kauaʻi to get ashore safely. Many of the people who could not get to the boats in time hid in mountain caves. The people who were caught were used as fishbait and human sacrifices, and their bones were used to decorate the *tiki* statues of the Tahitian gods.

The Tahitians who became the rulers of our islands called themselves *na aliʻi* (the rulers or chiefs) and they called our people *Mana hune* (small power) because they thought we were a joke. In fact the people who lived here before the *aliʻi* came were much smaller than these warriors, and had no knowledge of how to use a spear of club or any manner of war weapon. The early people had used their minds to cooperate with the world and had no war leaders or chiefs to lead them into battle. They were fishermen and farmers. They shared all they grew and caught with the community. To be a warrior you must be trained in the ways of war. No one in our Islands had such training at that time. Since the Tahitians did not consider mind power to be power at all, the people were as they said - *Mana hune* (small power).

Some of the people who were living in the Islands at that time were the descendants of Menehune, a man who had 16 sons. The two names merged and all people who were here before the Tahitians took over our islands were called the Menehune. In truth there were many different lines of families before the Tahitians. As a group they called themselves the Mu and the Islands the Mu also. Individually family groups were known by their own name. On Kauaʻi there was the Kama kau po and the Nawao. On Oʻahu the Lae and Pae and Kea families. On Maui there were the Ahu and the I families as well as many Lae family members. Some families were just known by their *'aumakua* and nothing else.

The people on Moloka'i who were my ancestors called themselves *Ka Po'e Ao Hiwa* (the light carriers, or the people who tended the Sacred Light). Other families on Moloka'i had names to do with the Light or the Rainbow.

Legends and stories of the Menehune's great deeds came about because the ali'i would give orders when they wanted a fishpond built, or a temple or a ditch, and allowed a very short time for it to be done. The *ali'i* would order the *maoli* (natives) to do the job and go off laughing. If the work was not accomplished in the given time, all the people of that place would be slaughtered.

When such orders were given the *maoli* or pre-*ali'i* came out of hiding – down from the mountains, from the caves – and they worked together as one person to accomplish the task. These jobs were done at night because during the day other work had to be done. When enough people were not available on one island, fireballs were sent up as a signal to the ancient ones on other islands that help was needed.

When the first rays of dawn began to show on the day the project was to be completed, the boats were already gone. The people had returned to their caves and mountains. There was no sign of anyone. Since the *ali'i* knew it was not possible for the people of that certain site to do the work by themselves, they thought the ghosts of their ancestors helped them. When they happened to see or hear people coming down from the mountains for such a project, they hid, for the burial places of the ancient ones were in the mountains. This is how the stories of the night marchers began. In those days, the ones who marched were flesh and blood. They would not bow to the rule of the blood thirsty *ali'i* so they hid away, waiting for a time when the land would be at peace again. Some families lived several generations in the mountains before they knew things would not change back to the old ways, ever again.

The *ali'i* people ruled through a system of chiefs. War was accepted as a way of life. They thought everything could be taken by force. They were always fighting—brother fought brother, father fought son. They had no peace in their hearts, and as it is with wars, no one won, for with wars, all lose.

On Moloka'i we were not bothered as much as people on other islands but we had our time of trial also. The *ali'i* feared the people who lived on Moloka'i for they thought all who lived there had great personal power.

The reason for this belief was that when Pa'ao's warriors came to invade Moloka'i's shores they found the people standing there waiting for them. They did not run. They stood together as a silent army. No fist was raised. When the warriors began to beach their boats the chanting began. It began small and became a mighty roar. The warriors threw their spears but they fell short of hitting anyone. Men trying to come onto the beach were falling back into the surf choking, unable to breathe. They did not invade Moloka'i shores at that time. They called Moloka'i—*Pule-o-o* (powerful prayer) and this was brought back into being many times through the centuries after that.

In time there was mixing of blood. The lines that had more of the pre-*ali'i* blood were called sacred and the chiefs who had such blood were called the sacred chiefs. Tahitians came to conquer our islands and in many ways were conquered themselves. They took many of our chants as their own. They took many of our teachings and our parables. Many *ali'i* came to Moloka'i and walked among our people as friends or family. They gave us no orders. Some of their children were raised by the learned ones on Moloka'i so they would know all things. Some of these men grew to be great chiefs. Some still saw more glory in battle than in awareness and love and their bodies died in battle for they had much to learn. Although some returned to their warring ways, others did not.

To us they were invaders. They took our women and our *heiau*. They felt free to walk among us and take our food or whatever they desired. They gave us orders and called us commoners. We were not commoners. We were the ancient ones who had lived here many generations before they invaded our shores with their red *malo*. They came to conquer with raised fists and war clubs. Many would learn new ideas and put down their clubs to pick up a simple bowl of light.

OHANA

Ka 'Ohana Kahua

THE FAMILY SYSTEM

Ka ʻOhana Kahua

THE SYSTEM BY WHICH THE FAMILY RULED

Although we lived in a communal society and much of the family possessions were owned by the whole community, each individual's personal possessions were treated by others with the greatest respect. A person's belongings were seen as part of himself and to trespass on his possessions was to violate the man himself. To steal from someone was to take part of his *mana* (personal power); therefore anyone who was a thief was expelled from his family. No mistake or crime (crime being a *haʻole* concept) was seen as worse than this. A person might suddenly become angry with another because of misunderstandings. He might strike out at someone, and a fight take place. This was understandable. To steal, one first had to plan, and the taking was a deliberate act against another.

The *aliʻi* put thieves to death; we did not. The fear of banishment seemed to work for us, for few were ever guilty of stealing. The few that were, during my lifetime, were frightening for me to see. They were told at a meeting of the entire family that from that time forward they did not exist. They would not be spoken to. They would be ignored and even if they were to walk among us, they would not be there. They were now *kauwa*. They were dead to us. In fact, they were less than dead, for we honored our family in spirit. The outcasts just ceased to be. Some of these people would throw themselves into the sea to die; others left and were not seen again. We never spoke their names, so we could not ask family, or people of other families, if they had been seen. This was an old rule of the family system and not challenged to my knowledge. This law of ceasing to be, was a very powerful one. We needed no other.

When a child was born, he was presented with a mat and finely beaten *kapa* by his family. These would always be respected as part of himself. As long as he lived no one would step on his mat without permission or touch his *kapa*. At times a person was given permission to sit or sleep on another person's mat. A person never crawled beneath another's *kapa*. Each person lay down covered by his own *kapa* covering. Whenever a person traveled — when he went to war, to the *Makahiki* games, on a business journey, or anywhere else — his mat and his *kapa* always went with him. When he died, they were burned.

For two people to share a mat beneath the same *kapa* meant they were married. When it was a love affair from a chance encounter a mat might be shared but not the *kapa*. Sharing a *kapa* had to be acceptable to both the man and the woman.

As a rule, the calabash or bowl of an individual was not touched by others, but there were exceptions. The elderly in the family were far more strict about their bowls than the younger members of the family. They had learned and seen people become ill from this, and considered it a bad omen. The sharing of the large poi calabash, and container of fish was done by all. It was only the individual small calabash that was *kapu*.

The elders of the family had several mats and *kapa* as well as their calabash. These were often cared for by one of the younger members of the family. With the *ali'i*, each chief had a younger brother or a son of a brother carry his calabash, his spittoon and his hair and fingernail clippings as well as his many mats and *kapas*. This person could walk in the shadow of the chief and the honor was tremendous.

Our family was not ruled by the *ali'i* chiefs except indirectly. We were ruled by our elders or *kupunas*, for they had lived longer and were wiser. Among these elders were the masters of the family—the *kahuna*. The elders of our family handled all disputes within the family. They also handled problems family members had with someone from another family, or with the *ali'i* chiefs.

The family colors were of the utmost importance to family members. This was true of our family and every other family: *ali'i* or *maka'ainana* (a person not of *ali'i* blood — literally the eyes of the land). Our colors were our identity — our pride.

To use the color of another was foolish. It could be the color of an enemy, or a line superior to your own and it would only invite trouble. To use a color that was not your line said you had no family pride. The family color was sacred.

Within the family all first cousins, sisters and brothers and half-sisters and brothers were simply called sisters and brothers. All of the generation of the parents were called makua (parents). All people of older generations were called grandparents. We called them *kupuna*. Individually they were called *Tutu* and their given name. We loved them all, for they first loved us. When you did not know the genealogy chants of your family it was extremely difficult to know which pair of these many *kupuna* were your individual line. To most of us it didn't really matter. A child did not belong to one set of parents but to *all* the family.

To tell our parentage, or the line of family, we used an "*a*." If I was speaking of my mother's line I would say Kaili'ohe a Ke-kau-like a Lunahine. If I was speaking of my father's family I would present my grandfather first and then my father — Kaili'ohe a Kai-akea a Pe'elua. If I did not know who the blood parents were I just stated the grandfather's name. Many people on our island had names with a Lae for the great line of Lae, many had a Kea for that line, and many used Mahi for the line of the Mahi chiefs. These were the three main lines left of the old ones, who had lived on Moloka'i so many hundreds of years before the Tahitians came to our shores.

When Kaui-ke-a o-uli (Kamehameha III) declared the Great Mahele and the land began to be divided among the chiefs, Gerritt Judd suggested to the king that all Hawaiian people be made to take family names. Many of the people did not understand however, and mix-ups were many.

Many people did not know who their actual father was and many questions arose around family circles and, in our family, a lot of giggling. It seemed so silly.

The Hawaiians believed that land could not be owned by an individual. They shrugged their shoulders when the *ha'ole* came to the Mission Station to explain what was being done. "More foreign nonsense," was the general opinion. When someone offered to give a few yards of cloth or a jug of wine for the title paper to the land many said "Why not?" The exchange was made. It was not that we were stupid. It was not that we were illiterate, for most of us could read and write. It was a total lack of understanding between two cultures. In our family, we collectively owned many things. Very few things were individually owned. The land, the sky, the sea, were for all men. How can you divide that?

With all these changes the old family system of rule was thrown aside and new ways introduced. The new ways, were foreign ways and useless to the Hawaiian heart. It left the Hawaiian without identity. He lost his family, his way of ruling himself, his history and his dignity in a few short years, all for the lack of understanding.

At the same time, the Hawaiian children were being taught a history in the government schools that had nothing to do with the memories of the *kupuna* (elders; grandparents) of the families. Government schools at that time were taught by the missionaries and their point of view prevailed. It was the view of the teachers from where they stood on the mountain. They did not see the Hawaiian point of view. In fact, in many cases, they did not see the Hawaiian at all.

The children of the islands were being taught that their ancestors were cannibals. This was *not* the case — not with the *ali'i* and certainly not with the pre-*ali'i*. The *ali'i* did have human sacrifices during the time of Pa'ao, and there were many during Umi's terrible reign. There were also many *ali'i* chiefs who put no one to death. Children were taught, however, that their ancestors were cannibals, lazy, and played all the time in the water and in bed. Teachers used the word indolent, a word never explained to me, but it had a very nasty sound.

I wish we had more hours to play in the water. I wish we had more time for rest and love-making. All of my life, my people worked very, very hard. We did not ask another to do for us what we could do for ourselves. We shared all we caught, grew and made. We wasted nothing. To waste or take what was not needed was great error and the person would be called upon at some future time to right the wrong.

It was my belief that the *'Ohana* system was the originator of what was later called the *Aloha* Spirit, for all life was founded on love. There was love of family, love of land, love of sea, and love and respect for yourself and all around you! All were one!

It was difficult for people to understand the family ways of yesterday. For instance, few can understand the fact that one household had so many wives. The Hawaiians have been talked about as if they had harems.

The concept of wife, and of family were very different from what they are today. It has always been the custom for Hawaiians to care for one another. When a man died what was to happen to his household? Who would care for the wives and children left behind? They were taken into the household of another (brother, son, cousin) as wives with all the rights and privileges they had in their own home. If they caught the eye of another, and wanted to leave, they had the right to go. As a rule, no woman was kept against her will. I know of a case or two where a man wanted very much to share the *kapa* of a certain wife newly acquired from the death of another. The woman would not accept him, and in one case when she wanted to leave to marry another, he was consumed with jealousy and refused to let her go. This was not usually the case however.

Some of these women were old enough to be grandparents of the men who took them into his household as wives. Then, as now, men want romance with a pretty face and a young, shapely body. Most romances were with beautiful cousins of equal rank, a comely commoner, or, to carry on the blood line, a sister to produce an heir of the highest blood line.

There were occasions when a brother and sister truly loved each other. Usually it had nothing to do with love. The sister would be kept isolated a month or so before the coupling took place with the brother. After that (sometimes before as well) she was allowed her own husband and her own household. That she was having children by two men at the same time seems strange to people now, but it was done in an orderly fashion. It was not a running from bed to bed kind of business.

When a man wanted to take a wife, but it left a sister alone, or an elderly mother, this person would be taken into the household also. Some of these women lived out their lives without sleeping with that man. Sometimes their stay would be a few months or years until they saw someone they wanted and who wanted them, then they moved on. While they were in the confines of his home they were called "wives." Women, *aliʻi* and commoner alike, always had the right to refuse to bed with a man. This pertained even to sisters who were to carry the blood line. Sex was not seen as something a man could demand and the woman had to submit. They were equal in the meeting and sharing of the responsibility.

Some women would flaunt affairs they had with high chiefs. A child born of such affairs was sometimes taken into the household of the child's father, and at times the mother too (not as a wife of any station, but the comforts were there just the same). High chiefs also used their high rank to claim the favors of young girls. Keawe-kekahi-aliʻi-o-na-moku (a high chief of Hawaiʻi) was noted for spreading his seed throughout the islands. It is often said that no man walks in Hawaiʻi nei that does not carry the blood of Keawe-kekahi-aliʻi-o-na-moku in his veins. With him, I think *aliʻi* and commoner alike were afraid to say no when he requested favors. He was a fierce warrior and not one who bothered with the feelings of others, regardless of their station in life.

There were many kind *aliʻi*. One of the best was Kamehameha-nui, ruler of Maui. When he died he passed the rule to his younger brother (not to sons) Ka-hekili, and technically, all his wives, and wives still in the household that had come from the household of their father Ke-kau-like, went to Kahekili also. Some of Ke-kau-like's wives had died and others had new husbands but some remained. Namahana who was the sacred wife of Kamehameha-nui refused to go. She had her own lands, kept her own council and kept the wives of Kamehameha-nui and Ke-kau-like with her. The reason she gave was that Kahekili who was now 59 years old lived too quiet a life for her. Namahana was full of fun and gaiety. She loved to party and gamble. Her household was full of guests and drinking all of the time. If she were to go into Kahekili's household all that would end. He lived a quiet life. He had two wives, spent his time swimming and surfing and did not even drink liquor. Kahekili was angry with her, for her lands by right were now his, for they had been his brother's. He had a few choice things to say about her, but he let her go her own way. Kahekili took no other wives when he became high chief. He once stated that had he known in his younger days that some day he would rule, he might have wooed a few pretty young girls. He was an excellent sportsman, but a reclusive man. He never drank of the *ʻawa* root, and he spent hours walking beside the ocean, swimming or diving with only one or two male companions.

Family, to us, on Molokaʻi was seen as a solid unit. A whole, of which we were each a part. In actuality, the family was a community or group of people living together, growing together, working out their problems the best way they could together, all connected, all learning and growing and assisting each other in their growth. We were all related in some way. Many generations — many fingers of the same hand; parts of one body.

Each *'Ohana* was governed by a group of *kupuna* (elders). Age alone did not make one a part of this group. There were many old people who were not. To become part of the ruling body of the family you had to be accepted by all of the elders. Everything was decided on consensus of opinion. The ruling body varied in size, and always consisted of *kahuna* (experts) of many kinds.

When a person proved himself through years of hard work and wise thinking, if they were known for being loving and unselfish in all things, and had mastered many of the family secrets, sooner or later their name would come up and the *kupuna* would discuss making this person a part of their group. No vote was taken. If everyone was in agreement, then at the family *'aha* (meeting) they were requested to join the other *kupuna* who ruled, on the upper part of the circle. It may sound simple. It was not.

One of the *kupuna* was our chief or ruling elder. He did not rule alone like the *ali'i*. All our ruling elders ruled together. This one person met with other family heads when there was need of it, and brought us news of what was going on in other families.

The *ali'i* had ruling elders, too, but they were not of the family line. They were the political supporters of the chief who had appointed them. These ruling bodies were called councils, and later after the foreigners came they called them the Privy Council. Most of the members of these bodies were men (for they fought the wars), but on occasion there were women appointed to serve. Ka'ahumanu was given the seat her father had held in the council when he died. Many *ali'i* women had served before in other councils, and the women who were regents after her death had important places in the council.

In our family line it was possible to serve in more than one family council. Maka weliweli served in her father's council before his death; she was a member of our *kupuna* (elders); and served in family councils for two of her brothers. Maka weliweli was a teacher and a mystic so was not always around when a family council was held. When she was with us she did not always choose to sit with the elders. If family members wondered why this was they kept it in their own hearts and did not ask questions.

Family members did not question the family council. The decisions they made were considered law and the family abided by them. They had the greatest *mana* and knowledge. For this reason they were our leaders. We did not argue with them, even if we disagreed in our hearts.

The *kupuna* ruled at all *'aha* (family meetings) and *'aha'aina* (meeting where food was served). They handled all disputes within the family and problems family members had with outsiders. When an *ʻaha* was called, no one questioned going. The rule was — if you were alive, not dying, or laid up with two broken legs, you got up and attended. It was not questioned; it was done.

At the *ʻaha*, matters of importance to the entire family were discussed, and once a year plans for the *Makahiki* were made. Family members were reminded of teachings, when it was felt that one or a few needed to be reminded. One teaching that people needed to be reminded of most frequently was: To say that one forgives and then not forget, is not to forgive at all. *Forgiving and forgetting are part of the same whole.* To say you have forgiven and continue to bring up the problem is a great error and is to carry a large rock in your "bowl of light." For the reason of forgiving and forgetting, many elders did not wish to discuss the past with the children. Starting to tell stories of long ago could often bring back old hurts, old feelings of resentment and anger. Stones long gone would arise again. Some who had moved on into the spirit world might be dishonored. So they felt it was best forgotten, and our history was buried with the *kupuna* and it was no more.

The *ʻaha* consisted of the flesh, or living family, and the spirit family. That a person had passed from flesh did not make them less family. They were spoken of and to, remembered in *mele* and chant. At meals they were remembered before the family ate the food. For this reason foreigners said we had hundreds of gods that we prayed to. Gods indeed, they were our family — our loved ones — our parents.

The *ʻaumakua* was also a part of our family circle, and explaining this is difficult. Perhaps you could understand it as a guardian angel. Christians believe that — well, we had our *ʻaumakua*. That is as near as I can explain it. The *ʻaumakua* was our identity and an important part of the family. It did not need to be in the body of anything, however, for the *ʻaumakua* was a spirit. They were like a messenger between the two worlds — the spirit and the flesh. They had access to both worlds (or places). Our family *ʻaumakua* was a *Moʻo* (lizard or dragon) my mother's family line had as their *ʻaumakua* the thunder.

If we were one with all things and all matter, we were one with them and they were one with us. Why should that seem so strange? Our family *ʻaumakua* were sometimes printed in *kapa* design on our family banner for the *Makahiki* games. It was to bring forth all the *mana* of the spirit family. Nobody was afraid. It was all part of the fun.

Our rules or laws were few in the family but we all knew them by heart. All were free to come and go, and do as they wished, as long as they did no harm to another.

All that was worked upon was shared with the family, divided into four portions; the first going to the elderly who could no longer work for themselves.

Who the elderly were, was not decided by any but the person himself. Some worked hard every day and were far older than some who had laid the day's work aside. Each knew his own heart and body. They knew when they could no longer share in the work load.

We shared with other members of the family and took the last portion for our own household.

Our family did not consider ourselves to be *ali'i*. We considered ourselves to be above *ali'i*. We were a sacred line, here from the beginning of time.

Once a year, at *Makahiki* season, we had presentation of family. Every family member who was alive attended this meeting. Family members that had moved away from our community returned. It was a time of great rejoicing, remembering and romancing — for we met family we had not known before, and the young ones fell in love, some stayed behind when the family left, while others left with cousins when the time came to leave.

At the presentation of family, each family line was presented and the genealogy recited of that line. With our family, all the children of my grandfather Kaiakea, their wives and children, grandchildren and great grandchildren would all be in attendance. This was the only time we saw each other all year, as we all had families of our own and the rest of the year we were busy with working the land and caring for the things that filled our days and nights. At these great celebrations all the old chants were told; of our history, our heritage, of *Moloka'i o Hina*. There would be many tears and much laughters. All who had passed into spirit during the year would be remembered, and chants and *mele* in their honor recited.

During this time, we did no work except for the preparation of food and other essentials. The days were full of games and contests. When the best of each game or contest was decided, these were the participants who represented our family against other families in the islands. This was mainly in sports, but included games of skill and martial arts. When the time came for our family to participate in the games against other families, we stood as one body behind our players. We cheered and yelled, and on occasion, when we felt a member of the other side did not play honorably we called him names and reviled his ancestors (for which we all had to be penitent later). Then as now, people were people. We had good times and bad times; fun times and hard times. The difference comes when it comes to family. Then we were part of the whole. We had our *'Ohana.*

Hakahaka Leo
O Haʻi ʻŌuli

OMEN READERS, SEERS AND PROPHETS

MAKAWELIWELI

Hakahaka Leo O Ha'i 'Ōuli

OMEN READERS, SEERS AND PROPHETS

Since the beginning of time there have been seers and prophets living in our islands.

Ali'i prophets were often part of a group that served the chiefs. Chiefs wanted a prophet close at hand at all times to consult in regard to wars, his health, his future in general and the future of his enemies. Some of these prophets only prophesied things the chief wanted to hear (would plant a thought), and the chief hearing and wanting these things to happen would act accordingly (*'upu*).

The *ali'i* had other prophets — that would not lie, but told things as they really saw them. Some of these were put to death for being so truthful. The ancient ones (the pre-*ali'i*) had many men and women who had been born with the gift of prophecy. These people we saw as special. It was our belief that these people were very old souls who had come back into flesh to help others. Sometimes this was a family member (close family) or someone of a far branch of the extended family (*'ohana laha*). We called these people *kaula*. It meant prophet, but it meant more than that — it meant pure energy — a true light carrier. Many of these prophets were also teachers. Around their schools (*halau*) and temples (*heiau*) they had many White Ti plants growing and Kukui trees. These were a sign to any who needed refuge, that this was a place safe from the storms of weather, or the storms of life.

Kaula were not people who would seek the limelight. You had to seek them out, if you had need of such a one. All were welcome at their door, *ali'i* and commoner alike.

Some of these holy ones ask questions, or requested certain things be brought from the forest or the sea to help him read the signs. Some had no need of anything except the question, and the truly great ones did not even need the question. Not all *kaula* found the answers the same way. Some shut their eyes and seemed lifeless. They would seem to not breathe. While in this state they said they could go to family in spirit, the future or the past to find the answer. Some said they would consult the family *'aumakua*.

The sex of the *kaula* was of no importance. Their ability, energy, and force was all that mattered. My own *kumu* (teacher) Maka weliweli was a great prophetess and seer. The greatest *kaula* in our family however had been Kiha Wahine of Hana, Maui. It was her name I was given as my sacred name at birth, because it was hoped that I had been blessed with her *mana* (ability-strength). Maka weliweli was to teach me the things a seer or sacred one should know.

On Moloka'i the term *kaula* was not often used, but then *kahuna* was seldom used either. Perhaps this was because we had some of the most outstanding prophets and seers of Hawai'i nei living on our island. Lanikaula of Puko'o was a great one, Kai-akea was perhaps just as great but in different areas, and his daughter, the famous Makaweliweli, were just a few.

When I was about 13 years old there was a memorable experience involving one of the elders of our family. I do not know the name of the prophet who was involved in this happening, but the incident has always remained fresh in my memory. My great-uncle had broken his hip and it would not heal. The bone doctor had worked on him but the bone would not stay in place. The elders sent prayers to our ancestors and all of us who loved him also prayed in our own way. Offerings were made at the family altar. The herb doctor gave him medicine so he would not be in pain but still he did not get well.

One morning my uncle asked that he be carried to the Kukui *heiau* in East 'Ohi'a. It was an agricultural *heiau,* but uncle had heard they had a great healer there. It was quite a trip to carry an old man but uncle was greatly loved, and his request was honored.

The elders chose four strong young men to carry Uncle Pu'u, and the elders followed behind. Food was carried for the journey, and mats so they could rest along the way. This healer was not of our family, and it was not known if he would see or help my uncle. Along the way the elders prayed. This whole procedure was most unusual. Family treated family. Everyone felt great suspense. Those of us who stayed behind tried not to worry but let the spirit family take care of uncle and the elders on their journey.

Uncle Pu'uolani had been one of the ruling elders of our *'Ohana* for many years. He was very aged, but his mind was quick and his eyes bright. Before they started on the journey he asked the elders to pick another to sit at the *'aha* (council) for him until he recovered. Pe'elua (my father) was picked, so he had gone with the elders on the journey to the Kukui *heiau.* It was from him that I heard the story in detail when they returned.

The trip to the *heiau* had been without incident. No one had called to them, there had been no barking dogs, the skies had been blue and clear, a high arched rainbow walked ahead of them. As they approached the *heiau,* a man came toward them. It was a strong youth in his mid-twenties. He told the men that he knew who they were and why they had come. He told them they had brought uncle a long, long way for nothing for his hip had already begun to heal. Uncle was old but he would live a long time. Then he looked straight at Manu, my cousin, who had helped carry uncle and told him to get his house in order, for his time was near. There was no way this young man could have known who they were, or why they had come seeking aid. They asked if he was the one they sought (for they had expected a sage of great years). He smiled in answer and invited them into the *heiau* for rest and food.

They rested that night at the *heiau*, with the young man and others like him giving them food and seeing to their wants. The next day they began the return journey home. Now that uncle knew he would live, he was at peace and quite merry. He did not feel ready to walk to his ancestors.

When people died and did not wish to go, or died quickly as in battle or some accident, they sometimes stuck around in spirit doing mischief. It was for this reason that we wanted all of the *'Ohana* to feel at peace when it was their time to go. The *'aumakua* was waiting for them, would make the walk easy for them, and make them welcome. It was the job of the family in flesh to help each other be at peace within ourselves especially when we were about to leave this life and this body. When someone (as uncle had done) stubbornly refused to go, we did all we could to help them stay.

We were taught from the time we could understand, that there are no accidents. All things happen for a reason. We may not know what the reason is at the moment, but we were told to always be happy even for misfortune, for with it comes some wisdom that we could not have had otherwise.

In Uncle Puʻu's case, he lived several more years. Uncle had some difficulty walking after that and used a stick or cane, but when he finally passed over, it was in his sleep, with a smile on his face.

My *hanai* mother and my cousins who lived with me at the *halau* felt perhaps Uncle Puʻu had to go through such pain so that Manu could know it was time for him to go. He was the young man who carried Uncle's leg on the journey and whose death was foreseen.

No one spoke of what the healer had said about my cousin Manu, but no one forgot it. I expect it was heavy on his mind as well. He made many trips into the forest alone and to the *heiau* at night, when it is easier to speak to the gods, and the ancestors. Manu was still quite young. He and his *wahine* (woman / wife) had three small children, a newborn at the time, a little girl was just learning to walk, and a small boy of three years. Manu was a good man; a good fisherman, a good net maker, a good bird catcher and a good father. He was quick in his mind, and kind and thoughtful of others. He was already being considered to join the elders when he grew in years.

One day as he was throwing his net way out in the water, he saw his small son trying to come to him. He dropped his net and tried to get to his son to save him from drowning. His foot caught in a bit of coral and he fell under the water. He and his little son took the trip together to join our ancestors.

In our family, many things were known about each other. That was how we helped each other. In the case of Manu, his death had been foreseen by someone not of our family. That was most unusual. That is perhaps why it has always stayed with me. All people are our family, are they not?

My teacher and *hanai* mother Maka weliweli was great in knowing the future. She taught those of us at her *halau* so that we could know the future and the past. She taught us to leave our bodies and search out answers. These were lessons that took many, many years.

From the time I was quite small I realized there was something different where I was concerned. No one was allowed to touch my clothing. I knew I had a sacred name that had great *mana* (strength or power) but I did not know what it was. Sacred names were not told to us until the family elders decided the name was correct. This didn't happen with some until they had been grown for many years. Sometimes the name was not told until the death of the one who gave it. Sacred names were just that—sacred, and not to be fooled with. Only one person alive could carry a particular sacred name at one time. To give a child a sacred name of one still in body was to welcome disaster to the child and to the parents. To name a child with the known name of another (one who was loved and honored) was done often. In this case something was added such as *opio* (junior) to show that this child had been named for the elder of the same name. We had many Kaili's in our family—all with different endings. My sacred name was mine alone and I would not know it until the time was right.

The tradition of carrying the name of some one of your family line, now deceased, was done if the elders felt a certain person had returned to flesh. At other times, it was to bring the strength and wisdom of that family member back into flesh (almost a "wishing it so" type of thinking). In cases like that, it was not always right and names had to be changed; sometimes because the name was too heavy (powerful) for the child to carry, and it could be seen by the family that the wish would not be fulfilled. In some cases, *Ka Maka o. . .* would be used. " . . .the eyes of . . .," adding the name of the one whose name they wished to use. This was a sly way to try to get around what the family in spirit wanted. In some cases they let it be. In other cases the wrath of the gods came down upon them and the name was hastily changed.

It would seem to a Christian that what a child's name was would have little importance, and yet was not their carefully picking out names from the Bible book similar to what we did? Were these not holy names? Did they not wish to bring the *mana* of that person and their name to this new child?

My sacred name was not told to me, for fear I was not the right one or would disgrace the name, or bring discredit in some way. When I was told my name I was 12 years of age and had just become a woman. This was actually quite young to be told my sacred name.

My fellow students at our *halau* gathered *kukui* nuts, polished them carefully, and on the day that I was dedicated, gave to me my lovely *kukui lei*. The nuts were uniform in size, polished brightly with the oil and fit around my neck perfectly. My *kumu* and *hana'i* mother, Maka weliweli, gave me a *lei* for my head made of *kukui* leaves and flowers. Now I, too, was considered a light carrier. My serious studies would now begin. I would learn the chants of our family. I had worked hard at my tasks these past years. I had tried to be humble; to listen and not to ask silly questions. I had tried to work quickly at the most menial task; to be prudent, patient, and always observing. I would now become a real student and be taught secrets I had waited long to hear. I was quite excited.

After my leis were presented to me, I was held by the hand and allowed to go up to the prayer platform where Maka weliweli sat to pray, to teach or to think. I sat facing my fellow students, and family members. Then Maka weliweli whispered my name to me and breathed into my mouth and onto the top of my head. To show emotion at this time was not correct. I thought I had not heard correctly. My mind seemed muddled and confused. The name she had given me was "Kiha Wahine Lulu o na Moku" (Sacred Woman — Keeper of the Islands). How could I bear up under such a powerful name? Tears were very close but from somewhere came a calm control, and the service of consecration continued without incident.

The known names in our *'Ohana* were crude and ugly. This was a common practice in the line of my father. Some of his sisters and brothers did not do that, but my father named all of his children names such as La hapa (half day — meaning shiftless or lazy), Ka'ili'me'eau (the itchy skin) and my name Kaili'ohe (the fetcher), but the saddest name was Ka ma'i wahine (the woman who was having her monthly period). The elders felt that mischievous spirits would not think we were worthy of their time and so would leave us alone. When I was older and lived among many foreigners I found their facial expressions priceless when we explained our names. You did not need to be a spirit to be turned away.

After the program of consecration took place at our *halau* a great feast was enjoyed by my fellow students, our families and our *kumu*. As important as this day was, the elders spoke of other things as we feasted that night. Things were changing in the world around us. Many foreigners had come to Hawai'i. Lahaina was full of them and more were coming all the time. They had been able to push Liholiho (Kamehameha II) around, but the family understood that, for he was an even tempered man and not sharp-witted. He was also easily used by any who gave him liquor. Now there was a new king, Kaui ke a o uli (his younger brother Kamehameha III) who had been raised skillfully under the wing of Boki and Liliha. Kaui ke a o uli was a smart man. He had been taught to read and write by the long necks (missionaries), he carried the *mana* of his ancestors. Why then was he turning against his own people? Why was he taxing us so highly? Why was he sending men out as friends, to snoop and see how many pigs and dogs each household had — how many fishponds, how large a garden. One family member told us that he had heard that all the money being collected went into the pants of Gerritt Judd, and he would allow the king only money for certain things. They said in Lahaina they called Judd, "King Judd."

The family was greatly troubled and talk went on until dawn. So it was, as I embarked upon my years of greater learning, the omens were already there, our world was changing around us. None of us spoke of the prophecy of Maka weliweli that they would run us over and stamp us out, but there were none among us who did not carry the thought.

When I looked back upon those days from later years, it was not difficult to understand. Our own teachings of love and light had made us vulnerable. We welcomed the foreigners with *aloha*. When they asked for this or that, we tried hard to make them happy. We did not know that men thought they could *own* things like land, or ocean rights. These things were for all to use. The *ali'i* parcelled off things for their own use, but with a new *ali'i* chief, these things changed. Our rights were curtailed only temporarily. The foreigners were not able to see or understand how we believed from their pathway on the mountain. We were not able to see how they thought and felt from ours.

We, on Moloka'i, believed in the light. We tried to keep our bowls full of pure energy and to light the paths of all who came our way. Our people had been taught by holy men who had come to our shore centuries earlier that there was an Enlightened One. They spoke of him as if the sun shone from his back, and the *ali'i* had copied this in their "burning back *kapu*." When the missionaries came they showed us pictures of Jesus. He was surrounded by light. The stories they told us from their Bible Book were full of loving one another. So, we all became Christians. I became a Christian many times. I found that I was also *pa'a* (locked into my past). I continued to go to the *halau*; to meditate and spend hours in meditation. I could see nothing wrong in trying to keep my bowl full of light. It was difficult for me to understand why the foreigners did not wish to see anything

from where *we* stood on the mountain. In my years of schooling at the *halau*,
I had learned my lessons well and knew you do not question the teachers, and
kept many questions in my heart. Others did the same. I was observant, however,
and I listened to what was said and what was being done. What the foreigners
said and what they did was not always the same. This was their "stone" and so
I let it be. My heart was often overflowing with tears I could not shed and I was
often frightened. One of the men who came to our island to teach us love, told
us that we should have only one man, yet he slept with my niece and she was
not his wife.

These new rules — these new laws — these new teachings — these new people were destroying us. The *ali‘i* with all their might had not been able to do what
was now being done without a fight, a war, or a wave of the hand. We were being
destroyed with ideas. Ideas that we could not understand. I tried to help those
whom I saw were sincere, and there were many but I withdrew from most
foreigners. I spent many hours removing myself from my family, calming the
fears that constantly arose within me. I must be strong! I must continue, for
Hawai‘i must continue.

The first year after my dedication, I was kept busy learning chants. There were
chants for everything. Chants to begin the day and chants to end it. Chants that
were said only at night and chants said only during the day. During that time
I began to realize why we had been trained so skillfully in memorizing fast and
correctly.

Family chants of my mother's blood line were far easier than those of my
famous grandfather Kai-akea. The Maui lines of the family and their descendants told of length of rule, age when someone died, things that certain people
were remembered for — great deeds and small — their wives, and if one wife
came from another line than the husband's, what that line was. These were easily
learned. The chants of the history of the early ones, the pre-*ali‘i* or *Po‘e Ao Hiwa*
were far harder. Some of the students of our *halau* had been working on them
for many years.

After a few months I found I even dreamed chants — learning in sleep to perfect tone, delivery and volume. During this time we were taught signs and the
meaning of signs. All our teaching intertwined like vines — the chants, the teachings and the meditation were as one. The long years of preparation in strict
obedience, paying attention to the smallest detail and not wasting time with silly
chatter, were now bearing the fruit of our toil.

We were excited about our lessons. There was so much to learn. Near the end
of that first year there was a feeling of unrest in our school. Our *kumu* spent many
nights on her prayer platform in deep meditation. During the days we could feel

the strain she was under. She told us that our lesson time was growing shorter and there was much to learn.

We continued to learn new chants and teachings. We also began to have lessons on healing and how to conduct *ho'oponopono* (how to correct) where it was needed. We learned faith healing, herbal medicine, signs to look for in a patient and what herbs helped which ailment. We took trips into the mountains and by the sea shore. These trips were loved by us all. We would practice our chanting as we journeyed. On more than one occasion, we would leave in the company of one of the older, more experienced students, leaving our teacher behind in meditation, and then find her waiting for us at the seashore or at a certain spot high on the mountaintop. I knew nothing was impossible, and I cannot say I was surprised. Now I wish I was able to do the same. That was not meant to be.

As time progressed we learned more history and lessons taught by our early ancestors. We were taught also in things we had always known, but had not been taught. These were called "'ohana knowledge." These were things we had brought with us from other lifetimes. We studied ourselves and why we had returned at this special time and place. Each person's lesson was different at this time. Each of us was her own teacher. We had to go into ourselves for every answer.

This was a time for self-knowledge. To be of help to others, we had to know our own failings and strong points. It was a time for self healing. We tried to keep ourselves in balance, for as our knowledge grew so did our power. Power can be used for good or evil. Temptations were many, and we could fool ourselves easily into thinking we were doing something for someone else, when it was to bring glory to ourselves.

As the years progressed, one fading into another, we continued with our chants and stories of the ancient ones. They were full of meaning and we loved the stories so it made it easier. As we became more knowledgeable about the past and its people, the individuals in the chants became alive to us. They were no longer just names in a chant. I could see why the family always spoke of family in spirit. They were so much like us in so many ways. I found I had favorites that I spoke to, and felt I often was answered, or that they were aware of my feelings. I could see many of them in my mind's eye. I began to understand them and why they had done certain things and why they felt the way they did. I fell in love with my ancestors. They were as much a part of me and of my life as the food I ate and the water I drank.

My last year in the *halau* continued much of what I had been studying already. My world had become much bigger than I had ever dreamed. I had learned to see things with my heart, not just the body "eye." I was beginning to view things in a different dimension. The understanding and knowledge that were to be mine were just becoming a small glimmer of what was to come. That year brought many changes in the world around me, that were not a part of my schooling, not of Maka weliweli's school anyway. Visits to the family circle brought news from our island and other islands. Two of my sisters had married. Some of our family had gone to Lahaina and others to Honolulu. Kaui ke a'o uli (Kamehameha III) was still king but the foreigners seemed to run the government. The family members who had been to the cities and had returned shook their heads as they told of the sailors and the goings on. There was much shaking of heads and everyone questioned everyone else about how could this be. What was happening? There was both the shock at how things were going in the city, and the refusing to believe that it could be so bad.

I could do nothing about it so I turned away from the things they talked about. I worked on my teachings, my lessons and my chants. I worked on my own growth. In dreams we had ways of telling ourselves simple truths. These were things we needed to tend to but had put aside or forgotten. Dreams were the spiritual self speaking to the body. Messages were often simple and to the point.

A journey in a dream was our journey through life on earth. This could be walking or riding a horse or donkey. You could see the person in the dream as someone else, but it was usually yourself that you dreamed about. When you dreamed of a person you looked up to, that was the good in you. When you dreamed about a person you did not care for, or did not trust, that was your own negative side. When dreaming of an enclosure, a house or small area in which you were confined, the dream was about your own body. It was important to pay attention to repairs needed in a dream. Dreams were what would, in later years, be called a roadmap.

Dreams were useful as ways to learn lessons begun in the day, and a problem taken to bed could be solved when you awoke in the morning. Forgotten facts could be brought to mind, chants and songs learned. It was very useful.

Dreams of flying were spiritual dreams. These were dreams beyond the earth state. They were of an eternal nature and of many lifetimes. It was a returning to the condition and place (state) where we were between lifetimes. We were with our spirit family.

As the Hawaiian people turned from their old ways, and became members of this or that "flock," those of us who loved our old ways and believed in keeping our "bowl of light," were watched closely. Members of our own families spied on us, withdrew from us and told on us. In all things we had to be most careful. There was division in the land and division in the minds and hearts of our people. It was a time of trial.

Ka Kahuna Kahua Haua

THE KAHUNA SYSTEM

Ka Kahuna Kahua Haua

THE KAHUNA SYSTEM

Types of Kahuna

Kauka ha'iha'i iwi	Bone setter
Lomi lomi	Massage expert
La'au lapa'au	Herb doctor
Niho	Tooth doctor
Kaukaukalolo	Tattoo expert
Wehe wehe	Dream interpreter
Imu (or umu)	Keeper of the oven (cooking expert)
Po'o	High priest
Kilo kilo	Reader of skies and omens
Kalai	Carving expert
Ho'o o ulu'ai	Agriculture expert
Nani i na 'ouli	Character reader
A'o	Teacher of sorcery
Kuehu	One who drove off evil spirits
Kaula	Prophet
'Ana'ana, Ho'o unauna, kuni	Those who used black magic (it was these kahuna that are remembered)
Ninau 'uhane	One who speaks to spirits
Haha	One who diagnoses illness by feeling the body
Kumu hula	One in charge of hula halau
Ho'o hanau keiki	Midwife
Ho'o hapai keiki	One who cared for women carrying a child; they were also inducers of labor
Mamake kaua	One who plotted and led wars
Pa'ao'ao	Diagnosis of children's diseases using hands (as haha)
La'au kahea	Faith healing
Haku mele ula	Makers of chants and music
Kalai wa'a	Canoe maker
'Ea	One who could raise the dead
'O'o	One who healed by bleeding the ill
Ho'okele	Navigator
Wanana ikeauokamanawa	Reader of weather signs
Kela moku	Expert seaman
Lawai'amanu	Expert bird catcher
Ka'a kaua	War strategist
Papa po'o	Leader of the warriors
Lawelawe iwi	One who cared for the bones of the dead
Lawai'a kolau	Expert catching fish with a net
'Upena hana	Expert fish net maker
Kukei'i wana'ao	Expert story teller
Hale kukulu	Expert house builder
Hui	Member of the chief's court who led functions and ceremonies
I'e kuku ho'ooki	Expert tapa maker
Ho'a 'ahu	One who supplied clothing for the chief and the court

The word *kahuna* was not often used by us. To place it in front of a title denoted that a certain person was the highest expert in his field whether in the *'Ohana* or on a specific island. The student who studied under such a one was not given this title even if he had studied for many years. It was not until an elderly *kahuna* was about to pass from life that he would designate who was to follow him. If a pupil was highly favored with wisdom and quickness of mind the *kahuna* would call him to his side, breathe into his mouth and pass on some bit of knowledge that had not been taught in the school. When the elder breathed his last, the new appointed one would pick up his duties. He who excelled all others became the keeper of the secret.

The term *kahuna* was not as revered by us, as it was later. It was any person with great knowledge in one or more fields. There were over 40 kinds of craft *kahuna* alone. There were 14 *kahuna* of the healing arts. There were also counselors to the chiefs — those who were the politicians. Since all the elders in the family were expert in many things, we were more inclined to think of them as grandparents, aunties or uncles.

The men who made canoes were considered by most people to be the ones with the highest *mana* (power) — that is to say, the greatest skill. Canoe making was learned only by a few to the point where they were considered *kahuna*. Craft people in mat weaving, coconut weaving, fishnet making, spear-making, *kapa* dyeing, *kapa* beating — were all considered *kahuna* when they became expert and could do things in their craft beyond the normal expertise of men.

The things we made were the fundamentals of life. We all learned to do many of these things. In those days we had no stores. What we needed, we made.

The word *kahuna* began to be misused in the mid-1800s by foreigners who did not understand Hawaiian terminology. By 1900 the word brought fear to many. There are always people who wish to trade on the ignorance of others, and these people found a good market among the foreigners. There were Hawaiian people who sold herbs as love potions and who used other herbs and prayers to end problems, or to bring pain or sorrow to an enemy.

In the islands at that time, there were many foreigners. On O'ahu and Maui they rushed to get potions with one hand, while they held their Bible in the other. It made the elders of our family shake their heads for those of our family who participated in such dealings. They made money, for they were well paid for their herbal potions. What power they had was lost — for they had lost the light from their bowls for the sake of fun and profit.

There were other *kahuna*. These were the priests that lived at the *heiau* (temple), the ones with the great power to tell the future, raise the dead, touch you and heal you. These people were called seers or *kaula*. They lived alone, or with students, and were only seen when someone searched them out. Today they would be called priests. They took no money for what they did. Still today, the test of a person being full of light is — do they charge a fee? If they do, beware. Those who carry the light help all people who ask for assistance. They, in turn, will be assisted by another when it is needed. Although it was customary to take food to be offered to the gods when going to the *heiau* (temple), it was not necessary to take a gift to the priest. They had farms and fished, just as we did. The students took care of the chores, and learned humility. Part of their training was to know all parts of life.

There were other kinds of *kahuna* who came with the *aliʻi*. These were the men who plotted wars, had men killed as sacrifices at their *heiau* (temple), and caused great destruction among our people. The first of these was Paʻao who came around 1250 A.D. These men were not of our people, and we had to keep them from the shores of Molokaʻi. There were times, when in order to protect our island from the forces of darkness, our people banded together and used all of our knowledge to keep those who would destroy us from our shores. It was at this time that Molokaʻi began to be feared, for it was seen by many as a place of great power, and that it was.

In our *ʻOhana* all who kept the rules of the family had great power. When rain was needed — rain came. When there was enough — it stopped. That was child's play and only needed good concentration.

Children in training in weather reading or star reading spent hours in contests of will, each concentrating against the other to make a cloud larger or smaller, to make it rain or clear up. Conditions would sometimes alter all day long as the children seesawed back and forth in their contests of will.

There were other contests of concentration: moving objects — sending them away, or finding them and bringing them forth. Stories of such things are now considered untrue. When I was growing up, it was everyday practice.

Life was a school. Life is still a school. People continue to learn as long as they live. The Hawaiian way was to believe that we had been born to learn, and we would continue to learn as long as we walked the earth. We had never heard of marching off to a building with a rice ball and a piece of fish for a foreigner to teach us about life. Our teachers were members of our own family. Who could better know our needs? The elders of our family were wise. By watching the children and seeing what they did well and what interested them, they helped us to place them with an uncle or auntie who could teach them all that there was to be known about a particular area of knowledge. Many children were placed at birth, or by the time they were one or two years of age, because they had already shown the path upon which their heart would lead them.

These children, because of signs at their birth, were given to someone to raise and teach in a certain craft or art. This placement was no more wrong than the placement of children when they were older. The *kupuna* (elders) knew what they were doing. Children placed at birth were usually the ones who were to be schooled as readers of signs and omens, navigators, or practitioners of the healing arts. Children chosen latest in life were the ones taught the history chants of the family. These children were usually being taught something else, and when their ability was seen, family chants were added. The history of the family was of great importance. The child had to show a good memory, love of detail and be able to sit for long periods of time in deep concentration.

In our family, after a near disaster when the young man who was learning to become the genealogy chanter died, the elders chose two replacements — one boy and one girl — to be trained. Thereafter, this was the custom. This happened long before I was born, but, because of it, my family knew the stories of its past, and I have the stories to pass on to my children.

Children who would study the genealogy chants were made known at a *'aha'aina ho'olilo*. The elders observed children under consideration for some time. When a sign was made known to one of the elders it was shared with the others. The sign was discussed and, if all felt it was right, it was time for the *'aha'aina ho'olilo*. At this time the family gathered together. The chosen child or children were presented and taken to the *heiau* where a ritual of consecration was performed. During this ritual the one who was the teacher would breathe into the child's mouth, and onto the top of the head and say, "May this *mana*, the gift of the *ku'auhau'aumakua* pass through me, and guide you." Thus the child's years of training began.

Up until 1840 all children of Moloka'i started their years of training with a ritual of consecration at the *heiau*. More and more, thereafter, this ceremony was carried on between the teacher and the child at the place where the teacher lived. This was due to the growing feeling among the people that to go to the *heiau* was to bring shame to themselves if discovered. By the turn of the century going to the *heiau* — by any except the very old — diminished. The young wanted to do things the *ha'ole* way. Many parents felt shamed by their children, so they discontinued old ways. It was not so much the missionaries that changed things on Moloka'i, as the younger generations.

Many of the people from Moloka'i moved or took trips to other islands, to Lahaina and Honolulu. They felt Moloka'i ways were backward. They laughed at their family's beliefs and way of life. Many of them refused to take part in family ceremonies, expecially ones held at the *heiau*. The leaders had lost their place of wisdom in their eyes. The young looked up to no one. For this reason I tried to keep my family from going to the city. I felt evil came in the cities, and had seen no good come from them.

My people — those who were living here long before the arrival of the *aliʻi* — had several kinds of *heiau*. We had fishing *heiau* — for good fishing and for the care of those of us who fished the ocean. We had agriculture *heiau* — for good crops and the care of those who farmed the land. Each school had its own *heiau* where the students asked their *ʻaumakua* for special care and assistance with their lessons. There were also *heiau* for Ku or Hina — our parent earth, sky and sea. Before the *aliʻi* arrived we had no wooden statues in or near our *heiau*. Later, under their influence, most of the *heiau* on other islands had *tiki*. On Molokaʻi this was done at Halawa by Kahekili and other chiefs put *tiki* gods at other sites on Molokaʻi. Our *heiau* remained as they had throughout generations before us. Our people, the pre-*aliʻi,* used the upright stone to designate the Father of all, Ku—and the prostrate stone to designate the Mother of all, Hina.

When anyone in our family found a stone that was long and smooth we would wrap it in a *ti* leaf and take it to some sacred place or to the family worship center. It was always considered a good sign to find such a stone. The rock had life just as we did. We felt it made the stone happy to be in a sacred place. I still think so.

We did not think of the *heiau* or the people living there as having supernatural power. We were taught that all things were natural. We were one with all of life — each particle of sand — each drop of water. All was a part of the whole.

All things were counted by four — probably because we had four fingers on each hand. When we took gifts to the *heiau* to put on the *lele* stand they were in quantities of four. One was for the earth from which the food grew, one was for the life-giving force, one was for the cleansing ocean and one for the purifying force of fire. It has often been said that girls did not go to the *heiau*. Under the *aliʻi* rule I cannot really say, but in our family and at our school we had a *heiau* and it was very much part of everyone's life. I had always been very interested in my spirit family, so I prayed to them, made offerings to them in thanksgiving for my blessing, and no one ever hindered me.

When I was old, my grandchildren and great-grandchildren informed me that girls did not pray, only the men in the family prayed; that the men had the right to put women to death for entering the men's eating house or any *heiau*. It might have been an *aliʻi* rule but when the *aliʻi* lived among us they did as we did. My grandfather Kai-akea had the reputation of disregarding any and all *aliʻi* rules he did not agree with.

The practices of healing were much the same in all of Hawaiʻi nei. The family *ʻaumakua* was asked to help bring about good health. Those in the family who were in the healing arts worked with any person who was ill. They would talk to the patient at great length about any stones they might be carrying. They would pray that all stones be dropped from the patient's bowl of light, and if anyone in the spirit world had ever been offended by the patient, that the person in the spirit world would now forgive the one who suffered.

There were times that patients were told that their illness was part of their learning process. This was to help them learn some lesson that they had, up to now, refused to learn. The lesson may have been of humility. When such a thing happened the family accepted it and helped in any way it could.

I prayed to Ku and Hina because they were our first parents, looked out for us and cared for us. I in turn loved them. I did not ask them to help me with my problems. If I had troubles, or there was a family illness or death I would go to my teacher and *hanai* mother, Maka weliweli. Sometimes I was told what was wrong before I was able to make a statement of what my problem was.

There were times when finding a solution to a problem was not easy. Trouble was sometimes caused by someone outside of the family circle. If the elders thought this was the case they had us all wear Ti leaf leis, called *La'i lei*. If this happened we all recited that the ill return to the place of its origin. "May the one who sent the problem or illness accept it back and free us from its grip."

If for any reason one of the great healers was sent for to offer aid, it was important that all signs be good. It was always best to not arrive before his meal for then he might not come. If he did come and someone called to him from the rear he might turn without finishing his journey or seeing the patient. Now it would be called bad manners but then it was seen as a bad omen. At such times when prayers were offered, they were sent to everyone. We sent them to the Christian God after He came, to the *ali'i* gods, and to the family *'aumakua* and all of our ancestors. At such times a feast was prepared and presented to the *'aumakua*. We prayed *O ke aka ka'oukou, 'o ka'i'o ka makou*, which means, yours the essence, ours the flesh. They got the smell, we got the food. Then the leftovers were burned, but the leftovers were usually few. Later I learned that the Chinese do this when a family member dies, and at other certain times of year. It is a small world.

Our family had a special *'aumakua*. It was called *Mo'o Kiko* and lived near the *heiau* in Kapualei. It was a giant lizard we were told and when I was small I had dreams of him. I did not ever see him. I felt no fear for if he was a part of our family there was no need to fear. Some said the *Mo'o* was Maka weliweli, and that she was a *Mo'o* I have no doubt, but I heard the story when she was alive. When I became old, there were those who called me *Mo'o Kiko*. I am sure they did not mean it as nice, but to me it was not an insult. I would smile. There is so much for us to learn. We are all so far from the top of the mountain.

Manawa Mau Loa Aku

ETERNAL TIME

Manawa Mau Loa Aku

ETERNAL TIME

In the early days, that is, before the Tahitian *ali'i* came to these shores, our powers were great. Our *koa* bowls were full of light and we could do all things. There were no laws of life or death in those days. That form of rule came with the *ali'i*. Our only law, if you want to call it that, was that all are one. Anything said to hurt another would hurt you also. You cannot strike your brother without it also striking your parents and your *'aumakua,* so it was best to strike no one.

In those days, it was commonplace for people to lie down, and their mind go elsewhere — to check out weather conditions, to see a loved one far away, to fly with the birds — or to find the answer to a problem too hard for the mind in body. This is still carried on to some degree, but far less. Now it is usually done only by a few, who have kept the light.

In those days, and after the *ali'i* came too, we could think people home. We sent messages to them wherever they might be and have them come home if we needed them. They always got the message and came home. The *'aumakua* would protect them. We would keep them in our mind, always safe, always well. We didn't worry. We knew they were cared for. The *'aumakua* could do many things for us like that, that we could not do for ourselves. It was a good arrangement, having part of the family here in school, the other part watching over us, and guiding us.

Our time was not of a clock. It was of the day, and of the night, cycles of the moon and the time of certain stars in the morning or evening. We had divisions of time, but nothing as rigid as a clock. Yesterday, today and tomorrow were one. We had been here before, we would be here again. We were here for a reason — to learn. Sometimes we had to come back many times to learn the lessons being taught. Sometimes we learned fast and could continue our journey on the other side, and guard and watch over the family in body.

There were many lessons to learn. One that seemed hardest for all to learn was that force of mind and force of the fist are never in the same body. The energy will go to only one.

It took time for me, as a child, to understand that the people who gathered at an *'aha 'aina* or *'aha* were only half of the family. The more important part, our ancestors, shared these meetings with us, listened to our problems and did what they could to assist us with our difficulties. Help was given to us in many ways. Our spirit family — who knew the way of the light so well, and knew the power and the problem of the stones — they blessed us, surrounded us with light, their love, and gave us dreams to help us understand and to learn, watched us fall on our faces, helped us up, and started us on the pathway of light again, and again, and again.

Everyone in the *'Ohana* had a high degree of dream understanding. From the time a child began to talk, his dreams were discussed with him. He was shown through his dreams, errors, and how to correct them. He learned of things past and things future, of body conditions that needed correcting, and warning signals of illness. Some dreams gave clues as to what a child would become when he became an adult, and names of all children came from dreams. No child was ever named without the spirit family being part of the naming process. The parent, a grandparent or an elder of the family would have a dream, and the child was known, and his name given.

We were taught four different dream levels. One was the physical — pertaining to all aspects of the physical body. The second related to members of the *'Ohana* and help needed, or warnings. Third were the mental dreams. In these, learning took place. Schooling began during waking hours often continued in these dreams. The fourth level was the spirit dreams. On this level people leave the body during sleep and travel. In those who were advanced in dreams of this sort, they walked to the other side of the rainbow and talked with their spirit family if there was need of it.

The Hawaiian people have always believed in many lives; in a continuing river of life. A life that flowed in and out of the earth plane, learning something new each time, always moving forward. Never being put back for mistakes, but given a time to think things through and then continuing on, correcting errors and making new beginnings. There was no word for "sin." We had to invent one after we were told we were "sinful."

This was a great difference between the Hawaiian beliefs and the beliefs of the foreign people who came to teach the Bible. They believed there was no river, no flow to life. It was a once or never trip. They meant well. They tried hard. They spoke love, they taught love, but they didn't *know* love. They taught "thou shall not" — and they were angry with us all the time for having fun and for the laughter and joy in our lives. They were not allowed joy. Salvation came to them only through misery. The Hawaiian gods were far more kind, for they loved happiness and joy as much as they loved sun and rain. They loved bodies the way they were made, glistening with sweat or with water from the ocean. They saw what we were, and it was good. The foreign God wanted every man, woman and child covered up and hid from themselves and each other. He was ashamed of his children. This is what the missionaries believed. I am not sure they were always right.

Jesus was a lover. He taught love. All the stories they told about Him were about love. He taught the same things we taught our children; don't kick unless you expect to be kicked back. Don't say mean things for words hurt worse than stones. Love the old ones, love your parents, love your sisters and brothers, love the babies. The more love you give the more you will receive back into your life.

The missionaries didn't always listen to the things Jesus said. The rules they made and lived by did not come from Jesus. They did not come from the Bible. The rules came from their own minds and hearts. They worked very hard at being Christians. It was a religion of laws and rules more strict than our own *kanawai* (laws) had been. I am sure their God loved them for all the misery they endured.

I too loved Jesus so I let the Hitchcocks dunk me and I became one of "their flock." I helped build the church at Kalua'aha. I tried to live like they wanted me to live. Many times I could not understand but they were older than I, they were the teachers — I was the student. I respected them. I covered my body, I did not drink of the *'awa* root, I didn't play in the surf on Sabbath but sat listening to sermons all day. I gave up many things that to me were pleasurable. I did not understand many of their laws, but I kept my questions to myself. Only once I asked a question. I wanted to know about the wives of Jesus — how many he had, what happened to them and how many children he had. Everyone was shocked. They said He had no wives at all. He was pure.

Pure is full of energy — not being full of stones. I did not see what that had to do with how many wives he had. Who cared for this man? Who went with him on his journeys and prepared his food? Who put his mats down for him at the end of a long day and massaged his tired muscles? Was this, then, the job of the disciples?

When Father Damien came riding along on his donkey and wanted to talk to us, we were happy to see him. We fed him and gave him a place to rest. I told him I already knew about Jesus and loved him very much. That made him very happy. The next time he came, he sprinkled people and blessed them and I had him sprinkle and bless me. It was a wonderful day. We were all very happy. Father Damien wanted to build a *hale pule* (a house of prayer). We promised to help him build such a house. We had houses for our gods, so we agreed he should have a house for his god too.

Father Damien was a quiet man who never yelled at us, or seemed to get angry at us. He asked us questions about why we believed certain things. We loved him. We all wanted him to stay with us but he always got on his donkey and rode away. He explained that Jesus never had a home or a bed, and, like Jesus, he would travel from place to place telling people about the love our heavenly father had for us. Watching him I learned about Jesus. They both were alone. No one took care of them. They had no *'Ohana*.

One day the teachers at the school and church at Kalua'aha heard that Father Damien had been coming to visit us, and that we were building a *hale pule* for him. Several of our family who had been "sprinkled" were summoned to Kalua'aha at once. The fathers and mothers at the Mission Station were very angry with us. They said he was not of love, but of darkness. They said his long coat covered a tail, and his hat covered horns. We were all very shocked. We walked home slowly talking about this problem. Maka weliweli had taught me truth was always the same — yesterday, today and tomorrow. What had been truth hundreds of years ago would still be true hundreds of years in the future. Now, I was being told things that confused me. They all carried the Bible Book. They all told stories of God's love and Jesus. They all believed in prayer houses and meeting on the Sabbath and keeping the day holy. Yet — one now said the other was not of light, but of darkness. By the time we reached home our decision was made. When Father Damien came, we would just lift up the dress (coat) and check his bottom. We would remove his hat and look for horns. If there was no tail, if there were no horns, we would know that he was of the light and we would continue to build for him his *hale pule*.

When Father Damien came the next time, there was great excitement, for even the youngest children had heard, and were anxious to see what was beneath the robe he wore. Before we had a chance to explain to him what had happened, the children rushed forward and pulled up his robe and thoroughly checked out his buttocks. They were nice and firm, and quite normal. We were all satisfied. The stone belonged to those who would have us believe in such nonsense, and the matter was closed. Father Damien had a congregation.

The matter of the time was one that was never resolved between us and the priests of either the Catholic or Protestant faith. To them everything was so very urgent. They were always in a hurry. I often wondered why they did not take time to enjoy anything along the way. We continued to do things when the omens were correct, and wait when they were not. It would be foolish to carry rocks from a certain beach to build a church, then have a big rain come and wash them all back to the beach again. When the rocks wanted to be a part of that church, when the sky and sea and surf were in accord that these were the rocks (or coral or *ohia* logs) to go toward the building of something, we would know. In the meantime, we had our daily chores to do.

To the Hawaiian heart there was the *Ao* (day) in which we did all manner of toil, for ourselves, our family, our neighbor, our old and our young. When the day ended, so did all work. No nail was pounded, no floor was swept, no hair cut, no dishes washed. With the setting of the sun, all work was finished until it rose again. *Po* (night) was spent in rest, visiting, remembering days of old, story telling; chanting and singing; in sharing time with our spirit family and in setting things straight around our own family circle. It was a time for joy and a time for love. It was the part of time that would ever be eternal.

Huliau
A TIME OF CHANGE

Huliau

TIME OF CHANGE

I might not have known which people were my blood parents, or cared, had circumstances not willed that all should be known. I was not raised by my blood mother, and children belonged to all of the family, not just one set of parents.

Grandfather, Kai-akea, was a man noted for many things. Ku-nui-a-kea Kamehameha had asked his advice and had him read signs several times. Grandfather respected this *ali'i* who had united all the islands and became king. Shortly after Kamehameha had received a promise from the Chief of Kaua'i that he would pay tribute and accept him as king over *all* the islands, Kamehameha sailed to the burial shrine of my ancestor, Kiha Wahine of Hana, Maui. There he made offerings and prayers of thanksgiving. He sent word to grandfather Kai-akea that he would stop on Moloka'i next as he wished to visit grandfather and would like to procure some of my father's fishnets.

My father (Pe'elua) was known throughout the islands for his strong enduring fishnets. All of the chiefs tried to barter for them. When he heard that the king himself wished some, he worked hard and long to make nets of the finest quality.

When the time approached for the king's visit, Pe'elua gathered his nets, gifts of sweet potatoes, wild turkey and yellow *kapa* for the king. The load of gifts was heavy and many family members went to assist him.

They arrived at Kaunakakai long before either the king or Kai-akea. As he was a younger member of the Kai-akea family it was his duty to see that all was put in readiness. Houses were built and a great feast prepared. By the time Kai-akea arrived, a large community stood waiting. Houses had been made of the finest *pili* grass with *lauhala* interiors for the king, his wives and retainers. Houses had also been built for all of Kai-akea's household, and for those of my father's house and other guests.

Kamehameha brought with him only two of his wives, the beautiful sisters Moku Aloha (Ka'a humanu) and the younger Kalakua (Ka-hei-hei-malie). Kalaimoku and his brother Boki were also in attendance. Both father and my grandfather were surprised that he had only chiefs and attendants of Maui with him. The Maui chiefs knew grandfather well, and our family was given great respect by them.

The young girl who was chosen to become my mother was in attendance as a retainer to the queen. She had been raised in Moloka'i and knew all the members of my father's household. During the stay in Kaunakakai my father fell in love with her and she accepted him. He took her to be his new and youngest wife.

After several days of feasting and visiting, Pe'elua accompanied Kai-akea and the king to visit the *maika* fields. My mother, who was caled Luahine stayed behind and acted as an attendant to her cousins. Luahine was young in years and had no high status among this group, so she spent her hours carrying and helping wherever she was needed.

When the men returned, all the king's gifts were stored on his ship, goodbyes were said and he sailed on to his home in Kona. Kai-akea and his household returned to his home in Kala'e, and my father, his new wife and family returned to Kamalo'o. Pe'elua was at that time 49 years old, for he was 50 at the time of my birth.

Pe'elua had two wives before my mother. One, Mai, (also called Ka'a kau'ele) was his sister-wife and the other, Ho'o pi'i was his cousin. She had recently taken a new husband, leaving his household without a wife.

Kiha Wahine, my father's ancestor, had taught that wars win nothing. She felt that only when men sit together as brothers can differences be resolved. When she died they made her a deity (a *Mo'o* goddess) and where she had lived they built a burial house (*puaniu*). This was at Hane o'o, Hana, Maui. Kamehameha I had an image made to represent her and had it carried with him wherever he went. He took her color of yellow as his own and pledged to her that if he united all the islands that the glory would be hers and peace would reign in the land. He made Ulu-ma-hei-hei-Hoapili of Maui her guardian and it was Hoapili who cared for the image that was carried with the king.

When Kamehameha came to see my grandfather, the image of Kiha Wahine and her guardian Ulu-ma-hei-hei-Hoapili stayed in the house in front of the house of my father. It was in this house of my father, at that time, that I was conceived.

I was born February 28th, the following year. On the morning of my birth the sky turned yellow and became very still. When I was born I did not cry but my hand flew out and grabbed onto the *kapa* of the woman attending my mother. Her *kapa* was yellow. So many signs said to our family that perhaps the ancient one — Kiha Wahine had returned. Only time would tell. I would not be told the name for many years. If I did not live in a way that would bring respect and good, the sacred name would be changed without my ever knowing what it had been.

My known name was Kaili'ohe (the snatcher). I was given at birth to my father's elder sister, the great seer Maka weliweli, to be trained in the ways of *Ho'opio'pio* sorcery.

Maka weliweli was also a famous prophetess. Kai-akea, who was her father, believed there was something special about her from the time she was a small child. She had a wing of white hair on the right side of her head (many in the family have since carried this mark). He taught her all he knew about weather signs, the ocean currents, the stars, omens and the meaning of omens, the clouds, the history chants of the ancient people, the chants of the family line of which he was so proud. This woman who had been taught far more than most, was now to be my teacher.

Small things are necessary before big things can be achieved. My early years were spent in learning perfect obedience. I had to learn to do what I was told and not be told a second time. I had to learn to listen and not talk back. I must learn patience, cooperation, understanding and service. These do not come easy to a headstrong young girl. Until I learned these things I could advance no farther. Slowly, very slowly, I began to learn my lessons. It didn't matter how small the task, I must do it without grumbling. During that time — not only in our school but in all of our family, children did not question or argue with the elders of the family. When they were told to do something, they did it. To question or argue was unthinkable. That was our way. It was from observing that we learned. We did as we were told and kept our mouths to ourselves.

Since all the girls and women at Maka weliweli's school were intent on learning and doing their best, I had many patient helpers along the way. The small girls copied the older ones. We learned that our purpose and ideals were the same, and we worked together as one body.

So often after I became old, and the *halau* (school) was no more, I was asked what magic I was taught; what potion did we use for this or that. The main lesson I learned at my school was not of potions, it was to see with the "inner eye," to see things with the heart. To understand the other person, we tried to be in tune — to the people, and to the environment. It was learning kindness and concern, not only for ourselves but for all people and all matter.

We were taught a value system that laid aside all material things. They had no value and were irrelevant. People, their feelings, the family, soul growth — these were the things that were important. Possessions were often stumbling stones in our pathway. We would tend to focus on them instead of what we were about. When this happened things got out of focus and confused.

This happened in my own family with my own children. Some of them learned the wrong things from the missionaries. They did not listen with their hearts. One daughter made a god of cleanliness. What about teaching them how to love one another? Her children learned to sit at a table with one hand in their lap and not spill a drop. When they were excused from the table they fought and screamed at each other. The children were not happy and their mother was miserable. She couldn't understand her children's actions.

Several of my children became involved with "things." One wanted the fancy things (possessions) she saw the foreigners have. She did many foolish things so that she could have these possessions. I was very relieved to see her decide for herself that she had been wrong and that these things, and wanting these things, took her *mana* from her and brought her nothing but heartache. A person cannot be involved with "things" and retain control of her heart and mind.

Changes on Moloka'i and the loss of light from people's "bowl of light" did not come about because of the missionaries. Foreigners had been in the islands many years when the missionaries finally came to Moloka'i.

Father and mother Hitchcock came to Moloka'i in 1832. Everyone called them the "long-necks" because their heads seemed to be so high above their shoulders. At Kalua'aha the king's mother had given them land to build a Mission Station. We were told to clear the land and build for them, whatever they wanted built. The land was cleared and a sleeping house was built for them as well as a large meeting house. This would be used as a school for sewing and reading and writing during the week and as a place for teaching the Bible on the Sabbath day.

I saw nothing wrong in believing in the old ways and believing in Jesus at the same time. Nothing they read or taught us from the Bible book or the man Jesus was in conflict with what I believed. Jesus taught that God is love. He taught that you should not hide your light under a bushel. He taught that seeds thrown on rocky soil do not grow. These stories taught the same thing we tried to teach the children.

One of my favorite stories was the one about the tax collector. Since the *ali'i* came to our shores, we had been taxed. That was a fact of life. Kaui-ke-a o-uli (Kamehameha III) had raised our taxes again and again. He sent tax collectors onto every island to see how much we owned. It was making life very difficult. It was hard to understand a man being a tax collector and harder still to love him. That Jesus used this for a lesson made me realize that no matter where people lived, or when, they had the same problems. We had the same needs, desires, the same light and the same rocks. It enforced all I believed and made me want to help these people from far away who came to teach us about Jesus.

Jesus was *kaula*. He had reached the top of the mountain. He saw all things and understood all the things He saw. He was where we all wished to go.

We all made many trips to Kalua'aha, but the missionaries made many trips throughout the island also. I was a part of all that went on. I helped when help was needed for I was unmarried and most of my sisters and brothers had families already. I studied to read and write. I learned to sew and make clothes from the cloth they sold us at the Mission Station. I liked the black gingham best. I could not bring myself to wear the white for many years. To me it still was a symbol of the 'ana'ana who had put so many people to death. They alone had worn white.

New people came to Kalua'aha from other islands, and some of the early ones left. I became aware that some of the new people who came taught love, but they brought fear. They lived in fear for themselves and for us. Many of the Hawaiian people began to fear also and their fear made them run from all of the old ways and beliefs. Family turned against family. I saw fingers point and accusations made when I went to the heiau, or the halau. When I went to sit on the platform and meditate at my school there were those in the family who sucked in air in mock astonishment that I would do such a thing, then run to Kalua'aha to tell them at the Mission Station what I had done. I was suspended as a member of the church after one of these visits. Thereafter I went at night, spent the night and returned at dawn. Had I spent the night with a man they would have only chuckled and wagged a finger. How strange things had become.

The joy of yesterday was slipping away. There was no song in the land. My people were trying to do and be everything the foreigners were. They dressed like the foreigners, they wore bonnets and hats like the foreigners, they even started to shake hands like the foreigners. Priorities were no longer the same. The elderly in the family were being passed by and not given their portion of food and other needs. The things that should have gone to the elders were now being sold by many or bartered so they could own things like the foreigners.

There was no work done on the Sabbath day. One day of the week we tilled and toiled for the king, so our work week dwindled. The land suffered when so many of the family members followed around after the missionaries to listen to them speak regardless of how many times they had heard the stories. The missionaries said "store up your treasurers in heaven," and many felt that they need no longer do their share of the family work. Jesus was going to take care of everything. I never felt Jesus said that. When he asked fishermen to come follow him and he would make them fishers of men, he didn't say, "you won't ever have to fish again."

Many of the remaining family had to work at night which we had never done —the night being holy. Some did not mind as they felt the night was no holier than the day, but working 15 to 20 hours a day can make a person weak and open to sickness. Some who had put down their work load, began to fish and till the soil once more. Things were not the same in the family.

The 1840s brought many changes. We heard in news from other islands that people called Catholics had come to Hawai'i. Sickness ravaged our land and my beloved *kumu* Maka weliweli died, Hoapili, the guardian for the image of Kiha Wahine, as well as Kalakua (Ka'ahumanu's beautiful younger sister) also passed on, the people had terrible fevers, and while lying in the surf, trying to be cool, drowned.

Ships with high masts sailed past our island constantly, going to and from Maui. When they wanted provisions from us they would anchor off shore and put down a boat for a few men to bring in the order. Many times they refused to pay for the provisions we took to them. Some of the Hawaiian men would swim out and fights would take place. Some of the women swam out also to stay with the sailors. The sailors were called *"Ke ali'i o ke kai"* (the chiefs of the sea). These men who rode the sea in ships had many things that the people now saw as good to own. Men sent out their wives to get mirrors, pots and pans, sweets, and yard goods. It being a much easier way to get these things than to pay for them with food or other things at the Mission Station. Unmarried women went to the ships just because they enjoyed the fuss made over them and the presents the sailors gave to them. Hawaiian men did not give presents or talk sweet talk, for they saw sex as a natural thing. Many Hawaiian women throughout the islands would rather be with a *ha'ole* man.

In spite of all the problems, our island was prosperous. We were sending *kukui* oil, potatoes (both sweet and russet) and many vegetables to California. It was easier for the people in California to get their food and provisions from Hawai'i than wait for them to come around the horn from the East Coast of America. Hawai'i provided California with its beef, pork, potatoes and many other things during that time. We began to lose men when they heard of the Gold Rush in California. Many left on ships for that far away place to get rich. Others went to Honolulu, Hilo and Lahaina to fill jobs of those who had sailed away to America. No family circle was left without empty spots.

About the same time we were losing so many men from the islands, the government decreed that all the chiefs should now own their land and be given title. Nobody understood this. At the same time the Hawaiian government decreed that the name of the father of each child must be published. It had to be put on paper at the district court. People could take any name they wished if they were over 18 years of age. If they were under 18 they *must* carry the name of the man who was their father. Some people paid no attention to either owning the land or to the matter of names. Others called themselves different names in different places, and some took *ha'ole* names. These laws did not seem to pertain to us. These were foreign laws made for and by the foreigners. We saw no reason to comply with them. Because of this many who should have been given land never got it, and some who got it didn't register it and lost it.

My father did not die until 1866. Pe'elua became his family name, his son Kimo took the name Opio as his last name. When Kimo was old he used both Pe'elua and Opio. Some thought it was two different people. It was just one. My father had 17 children, yet only Ka'aola, his son by Ka'akau'ele was to carry Pe'elua as a family name.

The schools created problems with names also. Many teachers would not call children by their Hawaiian names and made them use Christian names. So in school they were known by one thing, at home they were known by another and by the law a third name. It was confusing.

In 1855 I married. My husband was not interested in the new religion nor in the things I had learned from my years at the *halau*. He did not think *ha'ole* laws pertained to him. He drank too much and stayed home too little, but oh, how I loved that man. He gave me a family of children of whom I was very proud. After his death I married Lukuna Ka kiko pua ua ua of Maui. He was a very religious man, quick to criticize the children and myself for the smallest infraction of church rules. The children found him impossible. He left us for a woman who appreciated his "good" qualities, and we were happy to see him go. I needed no man to bring up my children. I had sisters and brothers. We were still family.

I tried to teach my children in the ways I had been taught. I tried to show them that Jesus was no different from what we believed. I tried to teach them to keep all things in balance.

They listened to my lessons as their eyes followed the ruffled dresses, the finery and the petticoats that everyone else wore. My words were often unheard. I kept explaining that *things* detract from soul growth and seeing with the "inner eye." Everyone seemed to be living by different value systems. It was safer to keep what I thought and believed to myself. Grandchildren were coming along and we welcomed them. I wanted to teach them; however, I found my grandchildren would not listen. They wanted to learn all the wrong things. They wanted to be clean (at least they saw it as good), to listen to their *ha'ole* teachers (and to disregard their elders and parents at home), they dressed and acted like the foreigners. They fought with each other and sassed the elders of the family.

I called my children together and explained that I could no longer stand by and see things continue to deteriorate. I wanted the children to know something of their past. I would not try to teach the chants but I would tell them the stories, the history that I had learned. I wanted them to *know love,* not just *speak love.* There is no God, where there is no love.

My daughter Luahine gave me her children to raise as my own, to teach in any way I saw fit. She had faith in me. My daughter Kaui said she would tend to the teaching herself. My daughter Mele offered to help me in teaching the children, and so it was. When the children came home from the government school, their school clothes came off and work clothes went on. As they weeded the garden, made mats, fished or picked *limu* (seaweed) they learned about the family. They thought I was a mean old woman for I would not stand for sassing or playing around. Each time they were taught something in the government school I made them tell me what had been said. If it was true from what I knew, I told them so, if it was not so, I told them that also. If it was something I did not know I looked for someone in the community who had been to Lahaina or Honolulu and asked what they thought about the facts. Then I taught the children. As the children learned, I learned also.

In time, other children of our family came to my feet to learn. I did not share things I had learned in my years at the *halau* with any but those I knew would keep them "in family" for we now lived in a Christian society. Things such as reincarnation could not be spoken and saying we talked to our ancestors was heresy. I tried to make all of them understand the Hawaiian way, the Hawaiian point of view. I taught them to be proud of who they were and of their heritage. I spent a great deal of time trying to correct the history of Hawai'i being taught in the government school. I continually stressed *'Ohana* to them, and how the family used to rule itself.

I was able to teach a few of my great-grandchildren before I gave up teaching. I saw some of my children's families follow the Catholic religion, while some were pillars of the Kalua'aha Protestant Church. Some became Mormon, and some stood beside me in believing there was truth in all of them and in the light. We all went to church. To me it mattered not where. God is Love and He can be found anywhere.

THE MOUNTAIN HAS MANY PATHWAYS

Ka Hopena
EPILOGUE

Ku, God, Jehovah, Allah, Inner Light, Love—one eternal truth. What does so great a power care what we call Him? Little minds put tags on things and people; Love accepts and encompasses all matter and all beings. Humans have been given the right to make choices—to be good or evil—to be gods or stones.

We are all born with that perfect power to do and be all things. We have the right to do with it whatever we wish. If we keep our bowl free from rocks, we can go forward and backward in time, walk with the angels, climb the heights and live in paradise.

It is everyone's own decision where and what he is.

We are all one, each a part of the eternal whole. There is no line that divides one from another or those in body from those in spirit. When men say they believe only this or that they put blinders on themselves. Blinders hide the beauty and majesty of what we are a part of—Children of the Most High! Inheritors of the Universe!

Life of 115 Years Ends On Molokai

(Special to the *Advertiser*, March 11, 1931)

KAMALO, MOLOKAI — MARCH 9 — After residence on Molokai for more than 100 years, Mrs. Kailiohe Kameekua, age 115, died at her home here yesterday afternoon following an illness of about a month.

The aged matriarch was born at Kaoio, Mapulehu, Molokai, on February 28, 1816, and lived at Kamalo all her life with the exception of short visits made to Maui.

Mrs. Kameekua, until a few years ago, lived an active outdoor life. She was an ardent fisherman, and was a notable exponent of Hawaiian domestic arts, particularly the weaving of fine mats, and making Hawaiian quilts. This form of industry she was compelled to relinquish about a year ago when her vision failed. Despite this blow she remained keenly interested in people and affairs on Molokai until her life ended.

Funeral services will be conducted at the family residence at 3 o'clock this afternoon. She will be buried in the Catholic Cemetery at Kamalo, with Father Henry officiating at the services.

Surviving her are three daughters, Mary Kame'ekua of Kamalo, Mrs. Annie Makakulani of Kalaupapa and Mrs. Kaui Paia of Honolulu. In addition she leaves several grandchildren and many great-grandchildren, several of whom were raised by her at Kamalo and Kapulei.

APPENDIX B

Statement Made by the 1880 Census Taker
In Regard to Moloka'i

". . . I went from Maui by ship. A short span of 7 miles, however, winds and currents being what they are, it took ¾ of one hour to reach port. . . . I was astonished to find the people there so prosperous, not affected by the "White man's diseases," and having houses made of wood, and living comfortably. They have large farms, fruit trees, taro patches and much fish. The soil there appears to be extremely rich. . . . At 'Ualapue there are sugar canefields, as there are at Kamalo'o. The sugar cane struck me as being very promising. . . . Large fish ponds encircle the Island with swells of thriving fish. Wild duck, Hawaiian goose, plover and many other birds are plentiful also. . . . I do not think there is a better place in the kingdom of man, than the Island of Moloka'i. These people are truly blessed. The view is splendid, the climate ideal, and I was want (sic) to stay awhile."

WEST OHIA

APPENDIX C
The Mo'o

The *Mo'o* (dragon) is very important to this family, as it is to all families of pre-*ali'i* lines. Our *Mo'o* is like the legendary Chinese dragon with one exception—it is a representative of time. It begins in tomorrow, the dawn that has yet to come. The eyes of the dragon look for a star to fix upon, always searching for guidance for the family. The front feet of the dragon are *Na Opio* (the young children of the family)—always restless, always changing position, always in motion. The middle feet of the dragon are the parents, *Ka Makua* (the solid force of the family)—the providers of the food, the home, the ones that take care of the young. Then there are the hind feet of the dragon, *Na Kupuna* (grandparents). These stabilizers are ever-prepared for anyone needing help—always full of *aloha,* always strong. Behind the *Kupuna* is *Ka iwi* (the bone or the ancestors) who have passed out of body. They help the family in ways beyond the physical realm—caring, protecting and guiding from the spiritual side of the Rainbow. Each position is in preparation for the next position—always moving on, always with the good of the family in mind. Each person is a small part of the whole yet each part is integral and necessary for the whole to be complete.

To understand how important this dragon is to our *Kupuna,* see how it is used in our language: *Mo'olelo*—our history and traditions; *Mo'olio*—our pathway; *Mo'oku'auhau*—our genealogy chants; *mo'opuna*—our grandchildren; *mo'owini*—a vision; and *mo'o waiwai*—to keep an account of something. So, *mo'o* covers all parts of our lives. We *are* the *Mo'o.*

PRE-ALI'I CARVED MO'O

Kamalo Area of Moloka'i

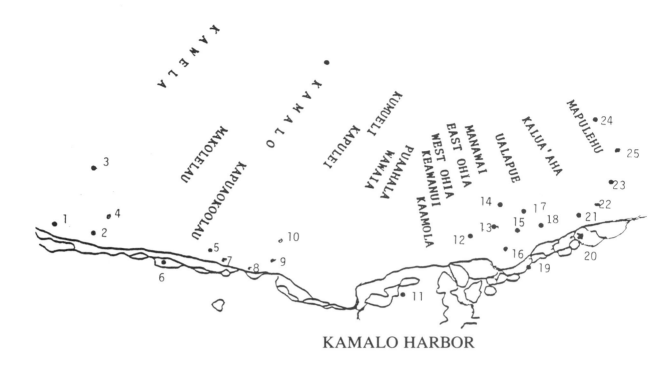

KAMALO HARBOR

KAMALO, MOLOKA'I

Moloka'i Sites Important to the Story

1. Kawela

Kawela was once a beautiful spot with lush green gardens and fruitful farms. In 1880 the census taker was quite impressed with the area and wrote it up in his report.

Kanoa Pond, Kewela, was a 50-acre fishpond in 1900, with a wall 2,860 feet long.

2. Battlefield of Kewela

The battle itself was called Pukuhiwa and was located midway between Kamiloloa and Kawela. Two great battles were fought on this spot: the first being in 1732 during the reign of Kamehameha-nui of Maui and Alapai on Hawai'i. Alapai was visiting with Kamehameha-nui at his home in Hamakua, Maui, when word came to the chiefs that the chief Kapi'ioho-o-ka-lani of O'ahu was trying to invade Moloka'i. Kamehameha-nui had been raised on Moloka'i and the place and people were loved by him. Alapai, who was the grandson of the great Chief Mahi said many who lived on Moloka'i were kin to him.

Alapai had with him his two war commanders, Kalaniopu'u and Keoua so he asked them if they wanted to go to Moloka'i's aid. They gathered their men and canoes and took off for Moloka'i, leaving Kamehameha-nui behind for he had just lost his father and was in mourning.

They landed at Puko'o and it was said the red *malo* of Alapai's warriors stretched from Waialua to Kalua'aha.

The fighting was in progress at Kamalo'o and Kapualei, and it was there the forces of Alapai joined the chiefs of Moloka'i. The problem in Moloka'i was that many of its men were holy men and would not fight. This left those who would fight at a great disadvantage.

The chief of O'ahu and his forces were encamped at Kalama'ula and Kauna-kakai. At earliest signs of light they were fed and ready for battle. For four days the fight continued without either side winning or gaining. On dawn of the fifth day the O'ahu chiefs made ready to fight when they discovered that Alapai had induced the men of Moloka'i to come and join the fight. They came pouring from every hill and house. The O'ahu forces were at Pakuhiwa and here the people of Moloka'i came against them.

The local people seemed to come at them from every direction and the forces of Alapai came at them from the sea. Those who landed fought shoulder to shoulder with the warriors and holy men of Moloka'i.

The fighting men of O'ahu drew themselves into a square box, with warrior protecting warrior on all four sides. Their forces were pushed into a smaller and smaller square and Kapi'ioho-o-ka-lani died at Kawela below Nakiloloa.

The taste of victorious blood was sweet, and on that day many who had previously followed the religious life sailed away to O'ahu with Alapai.

3. Pu'uhonua at Kawela (Place of Refuge at Kawela)

The fortification is high on the ridge that separates West and East Kawela gulches. It's up about 450 feet. There is a flat top and it is approximately 100 ft. square. Walls remain on all four sides. Within the great exterior wall there are several enclosures, one being a *heiau*.

4. Burial Mounds — Kawela

On the Eastern section of Kawela are the burial mounds of all who died in the great battle there. These were from the forces of Alapai, the warriors of O'ahu and men of Moloka'i.

5. Kamalo (formerly called Kamalo'o)

The families who descend from Kai-akea have great bonds with this land. It was here that Pe'elua set up his household. It is here the *heiau* Ka'apahu stands (over 3,500 feet up the mountain).

It is in Kamalo where the lava tube runs through the island to Pelekuna where the people could go to be in safety if trouble arose.

The winds of 'Ekahanui are named for the place by the same name near the head of Lepelepe gulch.

There are many small *heiau* in the area which were made by different branches (descendants) of Kai-akea. Most of these were Ku and Hina *heiau* and were for thanksgiving and prayer. There were no *Tiki* although some originally had *Mo'o* images as this was a *Mo'o* family.

6. The Mo'o Pond

Near the Kamalo wharf was the *Mo'o* pond. Many who are alive today remember the stirring of the water and the healings that took place there. Certain elders would speak to the water and it became calm — then water taken from the pond and poured over the person ailing brought back vigorous health.

7. Pu'u mo'o Heiau

This *heiau* was used for consecration of children and for family council. It has a L-shaped platform where the elders sat. The upper areas are covered with smooth river stones.

8. St. Joseph's Church

Kailiʻohe, Mele Ah Tim, Joe Kahaʻi, and many other family members are buried at this church.

St. Joseph's was built upon request by the circuit priest Father Damien. He would come to preach once a month and everyone brough their mats and listened to his stories of God's love and about the man Jesus. Many who listened in these early days thought God was Ku and Mary was Hina (the mother of all). He told stories of a great flood and devastation to the world and other stories that the Hawaiian people had also.

After they were clear in their minds that he was a man of God and not of the devil (as the missionaries at Kaluaʻaha stated), they built churches for him wherever he wished. These churches were not large, or made of coral as the mission at Kaluaʻaha. They were simple, small wooden structures. As the people of Molokaʻi learned to build the churches they decided to have houses of wood themselves and in the years following the building of the churches for Father Damien, most of the residents of Molokaʻi built themselves wooden houses also. The church of St. Joseph at Kamalo was finished and consecrated in 1876. Many area residents attended this church while attending other churches also. Some became ardent Catholics.

When the census taker came to Molokaʻi in 1880, he wrote in great detail of the beautiful gardens and quaint little wooden house communities that clustered around the Catholic churches.

Members of St. Joseph were very active participants in working at the settlement of Kalaupapa. Many made the long journey down to help during the week, returning home on week-ends. They made special foods to be taken to the elderly and the sick. They made a special food for Father Damien that he liked very much called "cookies." The church members who were free went down and helped with the care of the sick. Some stayed as *kokua*. The congregation was one of active participation.

9. Kapualei (now called Kapulei)

This land is greatly loved by the families who descend from Kai-akea. It was here that Kaʻa kau Maka weliweli started her school of sorcery, and the land of the entire *ahupuaʻa* was given in 1783 to her by Kahekili when she prophesied for him and the things she said came true.

Some of this land has been held by family members since that time. The land itself is dedicated to the *Moʻo* who is the *ʻaumakua* for the Peʻelua, Opio, Leonui, Kameʻekua, Kanahele, and Kekino families.

It was to Kapualei that Kaʻa kau Maka weliweli brought the Kalai Pahoa gods at the death of Kai-akea. It is the heart of the family.

10. Kapualei Heiau

Located on the Eastern side of Kapualei gulch. It has a small walled structure that has two compartments, where Ka'a kau Maka weliweli kept the gods Pua and Kapo.

On the mauka side of the *heiau* is a raised rock platform, 20 ft. by 20 ft. square. It was here that Ka'a kau Maka weliweli sat to teach and to meditate. The area was divided into areas where the novices lived and learned and the upper area where the more advanced students lived.

On the upper level but near the novice area is the tomb built for Ka'a kau maka weliweli when she died in 1840. In graves around her are buried some of her students and family who wanted to stay near her in death, as in life.

11. Kalaeloa Harbor

This is a natural harbor without reef or coral, which at one time was quite famous.

12. Heiau — West 'Ohi'a

There is no known name of this *heiau*, which is located between the stream and the boundary line of Keawanui at about the hundred-foot level. It is rectangular in plan, measuring 120 feet each way, enclosed with walls which are more than a foot thick. There are many terraces, the lower ones made for cultivation. The *heiau* was originally constructed with great care and thought, for when it was seen in 1959 by the Bishop Museum people, it was in excellent condition, despite its ancient (pre-*ali'i*) origin.

About 200 yards south of this *heiau* is another larger *heiau* which is also ancient. It is a rambling structure and was originally made of coral, with stones added to it at a later time. It is 50 feet deep. It is believed these two *heiau* were used together. One perhaps as a living site, the other a school or temple.

13. Kukui Heiau, East 'Ohi'a

Located in East 'Ohi'a on the low ground adjoining the government road is one of the earliest *heiau* of the pre-*ali'i* people. It was originally 170 feet long and 120 feet wide, and runs generally in a north and south direction.

Kaili'ohe told of her father and others in the family taking an elder who was ailing to this *heiau*. The holy one who resided there told them to take him home, for he was not yet ready to die, but the man who helped carry him (a strong young man, who seemed in excellent health) would die soon. This event happened as predicted shortly afterwards when the youth ran to save his small son in the water, caught his foot in the coral, and drowned.

14. Paku'i Heiau, Manawai and Kahananui

A *heiau* constructed in the traditional pre-*ali'i* manner. It was dedicated to Hina and destroyed in the time of Kamehameha. Kamakau say Paku'i was a *puʻukaua* fortress. It is located on the ridge which is the boundary line of Manawai and Kahananui. The base of the structure might be described as an earthen terrace, with retaining walls of stone. The terrace ridge slopes to the south. This was once surrounded by White Ti and Kukui trees because the grave of a great seer is thought to be here. This is perhaps also the burial site of Kapiʻi ohookalani who invaded Molokaʻi and was killed at Kawela. In that case the White Ti were not appropriate. The Ti and Kukui tree probably dated from a much earlier time.

15. Kahokukano Heiau, Manawai

This *heiau* is located on the ridge which is the boundary line of Manawai and Kahananui. Stokes described it: "a structure of 4 terraces following down the ridge. The 2 upper terraces are protected by walls on the west, north and east, and the latter wall continues along the third terrace. All of the other sides are open. The pavements of the terraces are mostly of large stones, many of them waterworn. In some portions the earth is found, particularly toward the northern borders of the floors where grading was done."

Connected with this *heiau* were the names of Kaohele, a famous warrior and athlete, and Kumukoʻa, a Molokaʻi chief and son of Keawe i ke kahi aliʻi of Hawaiʻi and Kanealae. Kaohele was a famous runner, and acted as guard and protector of the other chiefs who lived at this *heiau*: Kumukoʻa, Halai, Mulehu and Ka-lani ahi i ka paʻa. This *heiau* was built by the pre-*aliʻi* people, and was originally a fish *heiau*.

16. Kahakahana Manawai

This was a place to worship the gods of *kapa,* as well as a place to make sacred *kapa* prior to the year 1819. This site belonged to the gods Ku and Hina, and was used prior to the time of Kumukoʻa.

17. ʻUalapuʻe

These lands were given to Kaʻa kau Maka weliweli by Kahekili in 1783. The land is described as being good land, once filled with taro patches and a pond. Maka o lehua is the name of the wind at ʻUalapuʻe. ʻUalapuʻe is said to have had a spring called Loʻipuna wai. There are many legends about this spring. Some say that people who drank the water died of thirst; other stories said that people died of thirst searching for the spring which would appear only to the people of this land.

18. Hale o Lono — Kaluaʻaha

Located at the mouth of the western valley, this *heiau* is 2,200 feet up from the sea. Local people said in the 1800s that it was used only for prayers to the *ʻaumakua* (family spirit) and was very old. It was also known by the name of Pahu Kauila Heiau.

KALUA'AHA CHURCH

ST. JOSEPH'S CHURCH
KAMALO

TOMB OF MAKAWELIWELI

KAOIO BEACH WHERE THE PEOPLE
STOOD AND CHANTED AS PA'AO
RETURNED WITH HIS WARRIORS.

19. Mahilika Pond, Kalua‘aha

This was a *loko kuapa* 13 acres in area, and had 3 *makaha* in the 1,760-foot wall. It was used commercially at the turn of the century; mullet was raised and sold there. The mullet raised here were famous throughout all the islands. The wall is now destroyed, with only the foundations remaining.

20. Ka‘ope‘ahina Pond, Kalua‘aha

This fish pond was originally made for and used by Rex Hitchcock, a *ha‘ole* minister at Kalua‘aha. It is an area of 20.5 acres, the wall being 1,700 feet long. Since 1933, three *tsunami* have damaged the wall severely, each time being repaired by the present owner. At the turn of the century, it was stocked with the mullet and *ahole-hole*. In 1962, it was still being used. This is not the original name of the pond; the original name being lost. Now it is known by the name of the man to whom the land was awarded by the Land Commission at the time of the Great Mahele.

21. Kalua‘aha Church

Reverend H.R. Hitchcock and his wife arrived on Moloka‘i on November 7, 1832, in order to establish a permanent Christian church on the island. The area at Kalua‘aha was given to the Mission Society for a church by Hoapili-wahine (the widow of Kamehameha I, and wife of Hoapili) who was instrumental in having the Hitchcocks come to Moloka‘i and owned vast areas of land in Kalua‘aha and Halawa Valley.

First the Hitchcocks built a house, with the help of native Hawaiians, then a school and, in 1834, plans were underway for a large coral church house that could be used also as an English school and as a sewing school.

The church house was made out of large blocks of coral hauled up from the beach by oxen and men, using a sling and sled to bring the huge stones to the church site. Many people who never became Christians helped in this enterprise; families from throughout the eastern part of Moloka‘i assisted in the huge undertaking. The first building was nineteen by twelve feet and was completed in 1835, with continual additions being built on until in 1844 the building measured 100 feet by 50 feet. In 1853, the original roof of *pili* grass was removed and a modern roof was put on instead. This was replaced again in 1917 with a more modern roof, since the early one was in bad repair. The church was still active until 1967 although with a very small congregation. It was hoped at that time that the church could be repaired and a safe roof put on the building. Plans for this were later abandoned.

22. Ke ana o Hina

Ke ana o Hina, "The Cave of Hina," is a spot considered to be one of the holiest spots in all of Hawai‘i nei, for Hina was the Mother of Moloka‘i and, some say, of all Hawai'i. In the ancient religion, Hina was Mother of All, and Ku was the Father. In all pre-*ali'i heiau,* only Ku and Hina stones were used. No *tiki* or *ali'i* artifacts were used. Hina was probably of the first migration of people who inhabited these lands. Today we call these people the "pre-ali'i" although they have also been called the *Mu, Muai Maia, Menehune,* and *Mana-hune* by other groups. It is a shallow cave, this cave of Hina's, measuring only about four feet deep and three feet high. Its length, at most, is about 18 feet. It was in this cave, beneath a ledge of lava on the eastern slope of Moloka'i nui a Hina gulch, that Hina lived.

The elderly ones, told Rev. Forbes of her in the 1830s, stating:

"She bathed in a pool in front of her cave. Before bathing, she prayed, and that made the water come down and fill the pool. The pool was screened with maidenhair fern. On a platform of flat rocks above the pool she dried herself and rested. When her hair was dry she would return to her cave. In front of her cave entrance there stood a Kukui tree. Whenever the tree died, or fell, another sprouted to take its place."

In 1936, when the area was visited by George Cooke, manager of Moloka'i ranch, a Kukui tree stood outside the mouth of the entrance. Early notable "light carriers" were buried around Hina's cave. It was too holy a spot to bury them in the cave itself, so chiefs, seers, *kaula* and sorcerers were buried in the area outside, around the cave. Kane-alai, Kai-akea and Lae are thought to lie there.

No one should approach the cave without first making the appropriate preparation. Before beginning the journey, bathe. Leave all stones behind, and go with a pure heart. Offer a gift of food or flower, if you wish, but back away, without turning your back on the Mother of Moloka'i. *La'i lei* (*ti* leaf leis) are always worn when visiting the cave.

23. Mapulehu

This was the birthplace of Kaili'ohe. The lands of Mapulehu were once a *Pu'uhonua* (City of Refuge). In the proverbs that Kaili'ohe taught, she often stated, "When the rainbow spans Mapulehu Valley, look out for the winds of Waikoloa (storm winds) which will bring rain and destruction down into the valley."

24. Kaluanui (also known as Kaulahea and Okolepohopoho Heiau), Mapulehu

This *heiau,* dedicated to Ku and Hina, was a *heiau* where offerings for a good crop were offered.

A rock about 100 feet southeast of the *heiau* is known as Hina's rock. A man named Kopiko was stooping at that rock and three priests watched him with his *okole* sticking in the air as he bent over and changed the name of the *heiau* to Okole poho poho (sticking out butt).

25. Iliʻiliʻo Pae Heiau, Mapulehu

Mokolaʻi's most famous, oldest and largest *heiau* was built by the pre-*aliʻi* people who migrated to these shores as early as 2,000 B.C. The stones that made this *heiau* were brought from the shores at Wailau up and over the mountain on the Wailau trail. The reason for this distant spot being picked was that these people who built the *heiau* wished all things to be in accord, and so would only bring rocks that were in agreement to be brought. They undoubtedly went to several closer sites looking for good signs to take the stones, before going to one so far away. In those days, any sign or omen meant that they must do as that sign said. If the signs were good — the stones could be taken. If the signs were bad, they must look for another spot from which to take the stones.

This *heiau* was once much larger. It measured 920 feet in length and stretched far across Mapulehu stream. It was a walled temple with at least 4 defined terraces. It was the training place for almost all of the early ʻOhana-type *kahuna* (as opposed to the later *Paʻao Kahuna ʻana ʻana*).

After the *aliʻi* migrated from Tahiti there were changes in religion, and at some date, probably the 16th or 17th century, the *heiau* became of a more acceptable nature to the *aliʻi*. At the time of Kaʻala uo hua, the "Light Carriers" were no longer allowed the use of the *heiau,* and it was taken over by *kahuna* schools who used *aliʻi* gods, and *aliʻi* worship.

There are conflicting stories about human sacrifices at this *heiau*. Some say after the *Kahuna ʻanaʻana* took over and *Tiki* gods were placed in the *heiau,* some sacrifices of humans were made. Others stated that this never happened. We cannot state either way with much credibility. Knowing that the island was kept isolated from the *aliʻi* for centuries, if it did occur, it was probably in the 18th century at the time of the wars between the Maui chiefs, the Oʻahu chiefs and the chiefs of Hawaiʻi.

Family Chart
Genealogy and History

(k) — *kane;* male
(w) — *wahine;* female
 m — married

1 PEELUA KOLOIAAO

It has always been thought that Peelua was named for the caterpillar but we have learned that it is not so. They were both named at the same time. *Pe'e* is an early meaning for secret or hidden. *Lua* is a cave or pit, and is also two or double. The original meaning of the name *Pe'e lua* was a double hidden cave. Peelua was conceived in a cave by a young girl who would meet her lover there, after their first meeting during a rain storm.

The story went that the elders of the family followed the man when he left the cave and he turned into a caterpillar—hence the child was named for the caterpillar. Until that time the caterpillar was always called *nuhe.* So now it seems they were both named for the hidden cave.

Peelua had several homes. One was at Kaoio, one was at Kamilo loa (where the Hotel Moloka'i now stands). One was at Kauna la heleha. This was the main compound of all the family of Kaiakea.

Peelua was famous in the Hawaiian Island chain for his workmanship on fishnets. They were very strong, and held up well. The last time Kamehameha ekahi came to Moloka'i, he requested some of Peelua's fish nets.

2 KAIAKEA

One of the greatest family members, and an ancestor to nearly all who live on Moloka'i and carry Hawaiian blood.

He was known to be an astrologer, an astronomer, to know all of the weather signs, to tell things from watching the animals, the wind, the clouds and the sea. (These were not so unusual at that time as most people knew these things to some degree.) He was a prophet without equal and was known as a holy man, or *pu'uhonua* (a place of refuge). He continued practices of long ago and regarded the *ali'i* chiefs as barbarians. He refused to have *Tiki* at any of his *heiau* and worshipped no gods except life, land, sea and sky (and these were holy to all people).

He traveled a great deal and had homes at Kualoa and Olowalu as well as Kalae, Kalaeokala'au and Kaunalaheleha, on Moloka'i. In his later years he built a home at Kaha Nui (Pu'u Kahanui) and it was here that he saw the spirit people.

He believed that all men were equal and felt sorry for the *kauwa* (untouchable). He said, "All men need a place to call home" and gave his lands at Kalae to them for a community. This was most unusual for this was sacred land; the bones of his ancestors lay there. This had been by tradition land that went to the highest ruling elder of the island of Moloka'i. By giving this particular piece of land he was trying to show that no man is higher than another, and none is lower.

He was exceedingly strong and vigorous for when he was in his 90s he assisted his sons in digging a well at Kalaeokala'au.

There are many stories of him. Most of them are to show that he was very strong in his belief that no man is better than another. One of these stories tells that he would not allow any *Ali'i* chief to drink water from a certain spring, until his own men of peace drank, then the *Ali'i* could drink their fill. If a chief pushed forward to drink first the water would disappear.

Kaiakea wore his family tattoo of identification and tattooed the back of his fingers to show he did not make war. It is said that he followed the teachings of Kiha Wahine of Hana, Maui (we do not know of any time that he lived there, or that they lived at the same time).

Kaiakea taught all his adult life. He taught all he knew to his children save how to destroy another. This died with him, for it was evil to destroy.

He was a very opinionated old man and yet greatly loved. How greatly loved is clearly shown in the story of his last meeting with Kamehameha I.

> "Kamehameha looked upon Kaiakea as sort of a father figure, grandfather or elder. He paid him the greatest respect he paid to any man. When Kamehameha ekahi came to Molokai in 1819, on his return trip to Kona, he removed his clothing and crawled on his belly to the old Kaiakea. At this meeting Kaiakea was in failing health (he died shortly after this meeting) and it is possible Kamehameha took this way to show his great love and respect for the beloved sage."

M. Beckwith, HAWAIIAN MYTHOLOGY, 1970

Kaiakea's wish to do things in the ancient way (to live in peace with all men) now barely survives, but the stories continue.

Kaiakea's first wife Kalani po'o a pele io holani was the daughter of Kukui ai makalani (w) daughter of King Kualii and of Peleioholani (k) of Kaua'i.

3 AIALEI

Nothing is known of her other than she was Kaiakea's mother and the granddaughter of Keawe Nui a Umi on her mother's side. Her father, Kawelo Peekoa, was an important person in a Kauaʻi family.

Kauakawelo ai kanaka (w) was her half-sister—same father, different mother.

4 AIKANAKA (k)

Born at Holonokiu, Muilea, Hana, Maui; died at Oneuli Puʻu olai Honua ula; buried at Iao Valley.

He was the grandson of Hele pawa (an important chief in Maui's history).

5 KANEALAE (w)

There are two spellings to her name and there is some confusion as to which is correct. She is the daughter of Lae a nui aka Kahoʻoioa Pehu and Liʻa Wahine Luahiwa (who also has confusion with her name—sometimes being only called Luahiwa, which was also the name of the daughter of Kanealae).

There is a story about Kanealae that her enemies caught her and tied her to a stake in Kapualei. They lit a fire at her feet but a giant cloud came and rained on the spot and the fire went out. The people untied her and let her go.

6 KANEHOALANI (k)

Some historians believe this story belongs to an earlier ancestor by the same name. We found another person by this name, but he was too early to have belonged to this time. Both men probably traveled to America; however, *this* Kanehoalani lived at the time of Cortez. Kanehoalani was known by other names. He was called Maui and Maui Paumakua (after his earlier ancestor).

His main home was Kualoa, Oʻahu. From there he traveled far and wide across the Pacific. The trip that we know the most about is his travel to "The Back of the Turtle" (we now call it America). Many Indian tribes have stories of the man who came from across the sea—the man who would not make war. The Zuni tribe proudly show the rock on which he stood and talked to the people. The Hopi nation (or tribe) say some of his men remained behind and are part of their own ancestors. In the records of Cortez' scribes we get the story we share here:

"Montezuma took his army to the shore of the ocean and there they rested. After they had been there many days they decided to return to the fight. As they readied to leave a strange sight beheld them. Afar off, coming from the ocean were many canoes. Montezuma was called and he studied the sight. 'They are not of my people,' he said, 'nor are they like the men of Cortez.' Everyone waited as the canoes came near. Montezuma's men challenged the newcomers, but the men did not respond except for one lone man to approach them with open hands. He was clothed only in a loin cloth and concealed nothing. By signs and a few words he explained that they did not make war. They were men of peace.

"The men stayed with Montezuma and learned much of each other's countries and traditions. They shared many stories.

"When the fighting between Montezuma and Cortez resumed, these men did not fight but bound up the wounds of all men and cared for them as their own.

"Montezuma was mortally wounded. The man they called Maui attended him until the end, treating him like a brother.

"Maui was not want to go [sic] with Cortez but some of his men did go—some of his men stayed with the Indian nation (Mexico). Many men from both nations (Spanish and Mexico) were want to go [sic] with Maui."

SEKAQUAPTEWA—Hopi Nation

And we pick up the story with David Malo who wrote:
"He returned bringing *'Ka ha'ole nui, maka alohiohi, ke a aholehole, maka aa, Ka puaa keokeo nui, maka ulaula . . . '* (big foreigners, fat cheeks, bright eyes, ruddy skin and stout form). Then he tells us the men were teachers and priests. Some perhaps were but with so many of Kanehoalani's men staying behind, he needed to replace them with expert seamen, so how many teachers and priests is questionable."

Hale Makua Kekino, who spent four years with the Zuni Nation thinks that an earlier Maui could have also visited Mexico and the land to the North. He says the Zuni tell many stories of Maui, but the time is much earlier and they have him spending years traveling up and down the coast of Mexico and California. These stories have to be of a different man, for they do not fit with the stories or the times of Cortez and Montezuma.

7 LAE

Fornander, Vol. II, page 26, states that Lae was a high priest. What exactly he means we do not know. We know Lae had much land on Maui, Oʻahu and Molokaʻi. His main home, or an important one, was in what is now called Kahala, Oʻahu, and his *heiau* was on the ridge above the place Kahala Mall now stands. His home was near the beach area.

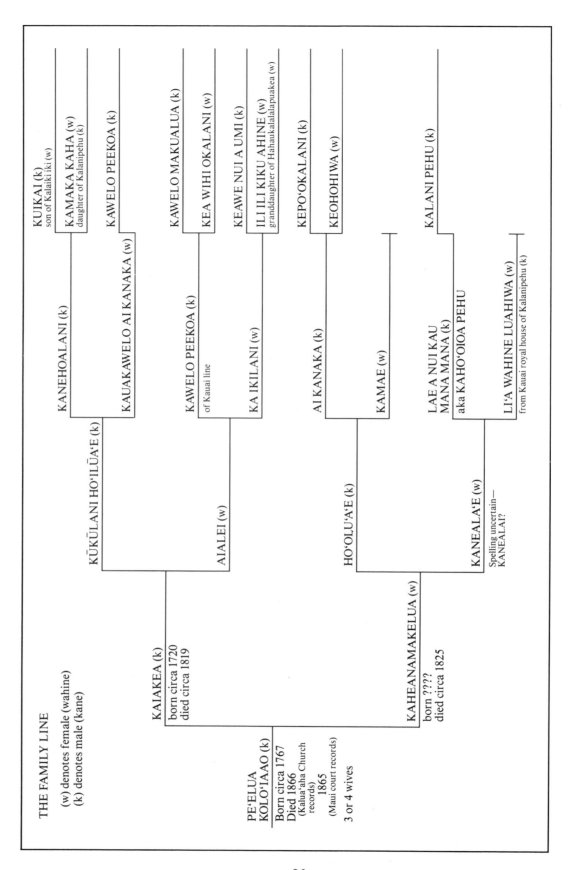

THE FAMILY LINE

(w) denotes female (wahine)
(k) denotes male (kane)

KUIKAI (k)
son of Kalaiki'iki'i (w)

KAMAKA KAHA (w)
daughter of Kalanipehu (k)

KAWELO PEEKOA (k)

KANEHOALANI (k)

KAUAKAWELO AI KANAKA (w)

KAWELO MAKUALUA (k)

KEA WIHI OKALANI (w)

KAWELO PEEKOA (k)
of Kauai line

KEAWE NUI A UMI (k)

ILI ILI KIKU AHINE (w)
granddaughter of Hahaukalalalapuakea (w)

KA IKILANI (w)

KŪKŪLANI HO'ILŪA'E (k)

AIALEI (w)

KEPO'OKALANI (k)

KEOHOHIWA (w)

AI KANAKA (k)

KAMAE (w)

HO'OLU'A'E (k)

KALANI PEHU (k)

LAE A NUI KAU
MANA MANA (k)
aka KAHO'OIOA PEHU

KANEALA'E (w)
Spelling uncertain—
KANEALAI?

LI'A WAHINE LUAHIWA (w)
from Kauai royal house of Kalanipehu (k)

KAIAKEA (k)
born circa 1720
died circa 1819

KAHEANAMAKELUA (w)
born ????
died circa 1825

PE'ELUA
KOLO'IAAO (k)
Born circa 1767
Died 1866
(Kalua'aha Church
records)
1865
(Maui court records)
3 or 4 wives

96

Polynesian Beginnings

(k) — *kane;* male
(w) — *wahine;* female
 m — married

Nu'u (k)—Lilinoe (w)
Nalu mana mana (k)—Mana mana ia kuluea (w)
Kaiolani (k)—Kawowoilani (w)
Hakuimoku (k)—Luikapo (w)
Nunulani (k)—Pilipo (w)
Honuaokamoku (k)—Ana hulu kapo (w)
Ne'ene'epapulani (k)—Wehekapo (w)
Hele i kua hiki na (k)—Hala ka po (w)
Hele mo'o loa (k)—Kawa na'au (w)
Ke ao a paa paa (k)—Ka ao o lae lae (w)
Luanu'u (k)—Meehiwa (w)
Kalani Menehune (k)—Ka mole hiki na kuahine (w)
Ka imi puka ku (k)—Ka ho'o luhi ku pa'a (w)
Newe newe Maolina i kahiki ku (k)—Nowe lohikina (w)
Kao kao kalani (k)—Hehaka moku (w)
Ani ani ki (k)—Kekaipahola (w)
Ani ani kalani (k)—Ka me'enui hiki na (w)
O puka honua (k)—Lana (w)
Hekili ka'aka (k)—Ohikimaka loa (w)
Ahulu ka'ala (k)—Mihi (w)
Ka pu'u lulana (k)—Holani (w)
Ke kama lua haku (k)—La'amea (w)
Lani pipili (k)—Hina i manau (w)
La'akea La'akona (k)—Kamalei lani (w)
Hawaii Loa (k)—Hualalai (w)

GENEALOGY LINE DOWN FROM
HAWAII LOA (k)—HUALALAI (w)

Oahu (w)—Kunuiakeakea (k)
Kunui a kea (k)—Ka hiki wa lea'a (w)
Keli'ialia (k)—Kahiki ali'i (w)
Kemilia (k)—Polahainaali'i (w)
Keli'i ku (k)—Keoupeali'i (w)
Kulani ehu (k)—Ka haka ua koko (w)

Papa (w)—Wakea (k)

This pair (Papa & Wakea) lived around 0 A.D. We find differences in different genealogies ranging back and forth 100 years, but they are very important people to Hawaii. Probably the elders of the family who settled here around that time, or a little earlier.

Ho‘ohokukalani (w)—Mano ulu a‘e (k)
Waia (k)—Huhune (w)
Wailoa (k)—Hikawa opua lanea (w)
Kakahili (k)—Haulani (w)
Kia (k)—Kamole (w)
Ole (k)—Hai‘i (w)
Pupue (k)—Kamahele (w)
Mana ku (k)—Hiko haale (w)
Nukahakoa (k)—Koulama i kalani (w)
Luanu‘u (k)—Kawa‘a maukele (w)
Kahiko (k)—Kaea (w)

Ki‘i (k)—Hina (w)   387 A.D.

(These are the parents of the twins Ulu and Nanaulu who were born around 400 A.D.)

This genealogy line can be seen in Fornander, V.1, Appendix IX, p.204.

GENEALOGY LINE OF ULU DOWN FROM
THE TIME OF PA‘AO

The parents were Ki‘i and Hina (sometimes referred to as Hina koula), year 387 A.D.

Ulu line—
AHUKINI—a La‘a (k) (circa 1210)—Hai a Kamaio (w)
KUMAHANA (k)—Kaaueanui o ka lani (w)
LUANUU (k)—Kalani moeikawaikai (w)
KUKONA (k)—Laupuapua ma‘a (w)
MANOKALANI PO (k)—Naekapulani (w)
KAUMAKA A MANO (k)—Ka poi nukai (w)
KA HAKUA KANE (k)—Manu kai koo (w)
KUWALUPAU KA MOKU (k) (circa 1420)—Haumeawahaula (w)
KAHAKUMAKAPAWEO (k)—Kahaku Kukaena (w) / brother
    and sister

KALANIKUKUMA (k)—Kapolei kauila (w)
ILIHIWA LANI (k) (1510)—Kamili (w)
KAUHI A HIWA (k)—Kueluakawai (w)
KAWELOMAHA MAHA IA (k)—Kapohinaokalani (w)
KAWELO MAKULUA (k)—
KAWELO PEEKOA (k)—
KAUAKAWELO AI KANAKA (w)—Kanehoalani (k)
KUKALANI HAOULU'AE (k)—Ai a lei (w)
KAIAKEA (k) (b. 1720–d. 1819)
PEELUA KOLO'IAAO (k) (b. 1767–d. 1866)

Peelua kolo'iaao had several wives and many children on Moloka'i and Maui. The children that we have verified are:
Lae (k) who married Umi (w)
Hainakalo (w) who married Samuel Kamakau (k), the historian
Peelua Opio (k) who married April Nakea (w)
Namealoha Kekino (k) who married Anna Ke (w)
Hosea (k) who married Maea (w)
Inaina (k)
Lahapa Hina'ea (w) who married Leialoha Mano (k)
Kamai (w) who married Leonui Ieke (k)
Kaili'meeau (w) who married Mauleia (k)
Kupihea (k)—
Kimo Kuhaimoana (k)—
Kaili'ohe (w) who married Kame'ekua (k)

LINE OF HINA (w)—KAMAUAUA (k)
who were the children of Maweke & Maiolaakea

Keoloewa (k)—Nuakea (w) these are brother and sister
Kapau a Nuakea (w) their daughter—Lani Leo (k)
Kamauli wahine (w) their daughter had 2 husbands:
Lani Ai Ku (k)—brother/husband, Malama i hana a'e (k) 2nd husband
Hualani (w) was their daughter who married Kanipahu (k)
Their son Kalahumoku (k) became the ruler of Hana, Maui.

Kanipahu (k) was ruling elder of Moloka'i when the Tahitians and Samoans came. (It is he who is given credit for starting the chanting that turned back the warriors.) Kanipahu had his main home at Kalae and it is there that he is buried. It is told by all the early historians that Pa'ao came to him and asked that he come back to Hawai'i with him and rule over Kona and Kohala. Kanipahu asked "Why did you seek me out?" "Because your *mana* is very strong," answered Pa'ao. "Go find my son Kalapana who lives in Waimanu with his mother Alai Kauakoko, and take him to be your king," answered Kanipahu. Pa'ao finally gave in, went to Waimanu and found Kalapana who agreed to go with Pa'ao and be king. He ruled with Pa'ao as his *Kahuna Nui*. We know this happened in the 13th century, and it is because of this that we are pretty sure of when Pa'ao came back with the legion of warriors.

From Kanipahu and Hualani, their son Kalahumoku m. Laamea
Their son (Iki a Laamea) and daughter (Kalamea) married
   and had a daughter, Kamanawa who married Kuaiwa,
   whose son Ehu m. Kapohauola
   whose son Ehunuikaimalino m. Keana
   whose daughter Ahuli m. Paula
   whose son Panikaiaiki m. Palena
   whose daughter Ahulinuika'apeape m. Koinoho
   whose son Kaili o kiha m. Hualei a kea
   whose daughter Mokuohualei a kea m. Umi a Liloa.

Kanipahu's son by Alai Kauakoko
Kalapana m. Make a ma La hana'e (daughter of Kamauli wahine and Malamaihana a'e) (see top of page)
   whose son Kahai Moe Leaikapupo'o m. Kapoakauluhailaa
   whose son Kalau nui o hua m. Kaheka
   whose son Kuaiwa (see above) m. Kamulei lani as his second wife
   whose son Kahou kapu m. Laa kapu
   whose son Kauholanui mahu m. Neula
   whose son Kiha m. Waialea
who were the parents of Liloa, the Sacred Chief of Hawaii.

Waialea, mother of Liloa had another husband, Kauhola
Their son, Kui Kui, was half-brother of Liloa
He had two daughters—
   1) Keakamahana, the great Kapu Chiefess and ruler
   2) Kalaikiiki, grandmother of Kaneoalani and great-great grandmother of Kaiakea.

We Come Together In Reunion and Aloha

November 1983 marked the 200th anniversary of when Kahekili gifted his land of Kapualei to Makaweliweli. Family members have lived there ever since. The elders decided that a reunion recognizing the Kame'ekua family would be held in Kapualei to honor that event. The *pa'ina* (party) would be on the grounds where Grandma Kaili'ohe had lived and where many of the elders had stayed as children. Committees were formed and many donations of food and help were given. It would be a *pa'ina* in the old *'ohana* fashion. A large tent was erected by the Mahi'ai family in the front yard of Kaili'ohe's old home. Family members came from every island and one from the mainland. In traditional style, the weekend began with respects being paid at the graves of Kaili'ohe and Makaweliweli. The island was toured by the family with elders sharing stories of family history at many sites and remembrances of events that happened when they were children.

On Saturday, a genealogy plus history night was held. Sanford Kame'ekua, the family genealogist, presented a large chalk board showing the lines of the family and explained why the family last names were all different. Then each family line was presented from the eldest to the youngest.

Sunday evening's banquet was at the old family home. There were few dry eyes when the chant and *pule* asked God's blessings on the gathering and invited all ancestors *(ka iwi)* to come and share in the celebration. Many family members displayed their talents by dancing, singing or playing music. Goodbyes were loving and sad.

It was not until November 1987 that the family would have their next reunion. This time the families of Kaili'ohe's sisters and brothers were invited to join the Kame'ekua family. This became a bigger *'ohana* named 'Ohana Peelua. (Peelua had been the father of Kaili'ohe and many other families in East Moloka'i.)

This reunion was held on O'ahu in a modern setting. Genealogy night occurred in Ewa Beach at the home of Greg Keliinui (one of the Kame'ekua elders). History and family lines were again presented. Huge boards encircled the backyard showing the family lines and where each person and place related to the whole.

The *pa'ina* was at Haiku Gardens and the entertainment was provided by professional entertainers as well as members of the family.

At this reunion, a new custom was inaugurated. It had been decided in 1983 that recognition should be given to people who live as "Light Carriers". It was decided unanimously that the first "Bowl of Light" award should go to Ray Lovell, a newscaster, who had traveled to Moloka'i to produce a documentary on the family's book TALES FROM THE NIGHT RAINBOW. Ray and his family were invited to the banquet.

During the program and meal, one of the elders said to the others, "Hey! Ray has become one of us—he thinks like us and understands our ways— let's *hanai* him and make him official." When Ray was called up to receive his award, which alone was a surprise, he was also received (with a standing ovation) into the 'Ohana Kame'ekua and 'Ohana Peelua as a *hanai* brother.

Ray Lovell was born in Knoxville, Tennessee. After attending the University of Kentucky where he studied journalism, he began his professional career as a broadcast journalist at a Lexington, Kentucky, radio station.

Ray was news director of a Lexington television station when he "succumbed" to the call of the islands—a pull he had felt all his life. He read every book, saw every movie and endlessly pestered anyone who had been to Hawai'i for more information.

Spring of 1970 found him as a reporter on an all-news radio station in Honolulu. Three and a half years later, he joined the news staff of KHON-TV, Channel 2.

On January 2, 1980, he married Karen Zane at Kawaiahao Church. They have two children: Mark Zane Lovell, born October 15, 1980, and Melissa Puaolamaikalani Lovell, who arrived on October 11, 1984. The Lovell children and their mother, Karen, are proud of their Hawaiian heritage. Together, they are learning more about the Hawaiian culture. It was this desire to learn that led Karen to read and recommend to Ray TALES FROM THE NIGHT

RAINBOW. Even as he read it, Ray realized he wanted to earnestly translate the essence of the book to a television documentary. He thanks Koko and Pali for that opportunity. Both Teddy Mahiai and the late Uncle Jesse Peelua taught him many things during the taping of the program on Molokaʻi. Ray is most grateful for the love and *Aloha* his family has received as members of the Peelua ʻOhana. Ray states, "I feel thankful for and respectful of the spirit of Kailiʻohe Kameʻekua who allowed us all to know her stories and feel her presence from beyond the night rainbow."

In 1989, another reunion was planned. Originally it was to be back on Molokaʻi but many family members had moved to Oʻahu due to a lack of job opportunities on Molokaʻi. Polling each family line made it seem more practical to hold the reunion on Oʻahu.

To try and maintain as much of the "old-time" feel of the reunion, many family members from a distance stayed the weekend at Camp Kailua. Family night was held there with Teddy Mahiʻai as speaker. He told of growing up among the old folks on Molokaʻi—being a "tag along child" hearing and learning many things that made no sense to him as a small boy—but which began to fall into place when he reached manhood. He told of the old farming methods and terracing the hills. He related fishing techniques and how to locate certain fishing areas around the island. He told of the *limu* farms and the crisp *limu ʻeliʻeli* that was famous at Kamalo. He left many with a sense of knowing and even experiencing some of the old ways.

Saturday was spent in "talk story" (visiting) and then traveling to Kunia Camp Gym where the families gathered for a banquet. Although the meal was catered, it was served by the Nakagawa family, descendants of Kailiʻohe's oldest daughter, Annie Luahine. Music and entertainment were provided by family members. The "Bowl of Light" award was considered for presentation to Theodore Mahiʻai. In discussion with the ruling elders, Teddy suggested instead that the award be presented to Pali Lee Willis in recognition of her time devoted to researching and compiling the family stories into the book TALES FROM THE NIGHT RAINBOW.

Pali Jae Lee, born November 26, 1926, was educated at the University of Hawaii and Michigan State University. On April 7, 1945, she married an old friend, Richard H. W. Lee. In 1947, he took his wife and baby to the mainland where he planned to complete his doctorate in psychology. It would be 20 years before Pali would return to Hawaii to live. Their marriage produced five daughters: Lani Catherine Lokelani Ngit Lan; Karin Elizabeth Kahalanani Wai Lin; Ona G. Ku'ulei Wai Moi; Laurie Brett Kehaulani Wai Chin; and Robin Louise Maile.

After her marriage dissolved, Pali moved to San Francisco, then home to Hawai'i where all but the youngest of her daughters were attending school or working. For a time, Pali worked as a research assistant at the Bishop Museum's Department of Anthropology.

In 1978 she married John K. Willis. In 1983 she left the museum to commit all her time and energy to collecting and preserving the Kame'ekua stories and history.

She is author of six books and co-author of two. She has been given many awards for her research and is listed in the Directory of International Biography; Who's Who in American Women; Who's Who in the West; Who's Who in the World and Contemporary Authors.

LILIA HALE & FRANCES LINKEN
AT 1987 REUNION.

JACK AND EMMA BAKER AT 1987 REUNION.

MAKA AHUNA, MUI LANG (KAME'EKUA LINE) & FRANKLIN BAKER WITH FAMILY,
1987 REUNION.

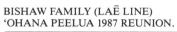

BISHAW FAMILY (LAĒ LINE)
'OHANA PEELUA 1987 REUNION.

Many of these facts have been known at some point in time, but have been forgotten. Some of these facts have never been known by Hawai'i's immigrant population (meaning from any place other than Hawai'i).

1) Hawai'i had a Constitutional Government in 1852. On January 11, 1855, when Alexander Liholiho was inaugurated to the status of King Kamehameha IV he took the oath "... to maintain the Constitution of the Kingdom whole and inviolate, and to govern in conformity with that and the laws." He stated, "You have all been witnesses this day to the solemn oath I have taken in the presence of Almighty God and this assembly, to preserve inviolate the Constitution. This is no idle ceremony. The Constitution which I have sworn to maintain has its foundation laid in the deep and immutable principles of Liberty, Justice and Equality, and by these, and none other, I hope to be guided in the administration of my Government."

2) Hawai'i had mail service from 1845 and, by 1848, it was frequent and fairly regular between Honolulu and San Francisco. In the Honolulu *Polynesian* newspaper dated June 30, 1855, it was stated a letter from New York City had arrived in Honolulu in 35 days. This mail route was not across the United States which was still mostly unpopulated but across the continent by way of St. Blas, and Mazatlan and then trading vessels.

3) The *Pali* trail was widened to become a road in 1845 and paved with stones. It was improved further in 1861 so horse-drawn wagons could journey back and forth. The road then called "the around-the-island road" but later called Kamehameha Highway was improved in the area from Honolulu to Ewa the same year. In a local newspaper it was noted in 1862, "Dr. Ford drove from Honolulu to Laie and returned in 8 hours."

   In 1862, a Maui newspaper stated, "there is a good carriage road on the island extending from Wailuku via Makawao to Ulupalakua, a distance of over 40 miles." A road was begun in 1849 on the Island of Hawai'i to connect Kailua, Kona and Hilo, which was the port town, but after several years of heartbreaking labor, the road was discontinued. In the early 1860s, an easier route was chosen and the road became a reality.

4) Hawaiʻi was considered a Christian Country by the Missionaries and the Mission Board from which they came in 1844, and missionaries were sent out from Hawaiʻi to other island groups.

5) The first printing press West of the Mississippi began operation in Honolulu, November 1820. By 1822 it was in constant use printing educational material for the schools and religious materials.

6) In 1834 two newspapers were established: *Kalama* in Lahaina and *Kekumu* in Honolulu.

7) By 1854 Hawaiʻi had the largest literal population per capita in the world. This was because the people went to school as a family. The youngest to the eldest went. Most of the population could read and write Hawaiian and English, although most did not learn to speak the English language until a much later date.

8) Hawaiʻi supplied most of the needs of the West Coast area: food, oil for lamps, and many other items during the "Gold Rush" days. The potato that became known as the Idaho Potato, and later was taken to Ireland and was called the Irish Potato, started in Hawaiʻi (Polynesia) and was one of the food items sent to feed the miners. The yam was another import, however, it did not take well, or there was not as much interest until later.

9) This Hawaiʻi that the tourist industry pictures as a quaint little group of islands peopled by ignorant savages, had an established government in 1778, and by 1800 had foreign trade with China, Japan, England, France, Portugal and Spain. By 1810 Germany and Russia also traded here. Hawaiʻi was considered a civilized country by all of them. Only the area that would later become the United States saw Hawaiʻi as "less than".

10) Iolani Palace was illuminated with electric lights on July 20, 1886. That same year the legislature appropriated money to light the streets of Honolulu.

11) The first telephone was established on Maui in 1878, and in Honolulu in 1879. The Hawaiian Bell Telephone Company was established in 1880.

12) To bring clarification to a long misunderstood tale, Captain Cook was not eaten. The Hawaiian, Tongan and Tahitian people never practiced eating human flesh. Captain Cook's body was prepared for burial as the body of any High Chief's body would be prepared. The flesh was removed from the bones as only the bones were preserved and buried. These were returned to the ship by the High Chief Palea, with the bones wrapped carefully in one of his own feather capes. Some of the

seamen *thought* his flesh had been eaten, although it was explained that was not the case. When the ship returned to England without its master, the tale took hold, and in a few years returned to be heard in Hawai'i. Many Hawaiian people thought this was funny, and instead of explaining to a person who had heard the story, that it was totally untrue, added embellishments to it, and enjoyed the horror of the person listening to the story. Such stories have not helped relations with our neighbors in America. There are many today who continue to believe this ridiculous story.

13) Where did the Hawaiians come from? Every tourist guide hears this many times a day. Even the theory that the Hawaiians came in 1200 A.D. (now disproved) would say they had been in one place longer than any of the curious seekers of knowledge. Most of the people who ask these questions may know who their grandparents were, or their great-grandparents; they may know that back there someplace in the past, the family came from Germany, Ireland, or England.

Most Polynesian people know who most of the ancestors were by name and many by deed and travels to the year 0 and some families even earlier. The *Mo'o* Clan have their family line from 800 B.C.

Still this does not satisfy those who ask the questions—*but where did they come from?* What some of us have finally realized is they want to know are the Hawaiian people from Africa? Well, since Richard Leakey believes (and his hypothesis is widely recognized as true) the first man was from that area, unless a person dropped from outer space, everyone originated there. In more recent times (3000 to 4000 years ago) Patrick Kirch, Anthropologist, University of California, Berkeley, who spent several years carbon dating the Pacific Basin areas, artifacts and home sites, believes that the Proto-Polynesian people (those who would become the Polynesian race) were nomads who lived on the sea, crisscrossing back and forth, knowing all areas of the sea as a mother knows her children. These people came from many places and brought some of their own cultures with them. Many came from China and India. It was a mixing back and forth, many of the people who became natives of Mexico and North America were part of this group, the Japanese and Okinawans also began at some point from a different place. The Proto-Tongic group were the first to break away and settle in one specific area. This he dates around 3500 B.C. The next 500 years saw a change with many island groups being settled, with permanent house platforms, irrigation ditches, terracing of hills, all showing the people were going to stay at this or that location. At about this time the first people settled in what is now called Hawaiʻi. Through the years many others would come—from the Marquesas, Tahiti, Samoa, Japan, Mexico, United States area (all of these places being called by different names at that time). So who are the people of Hawaiʻi? Where did they come from? They are the family of man. They came from everywhere. They are everyone. They are the people who learned you could live with *Aloha,* that man could live in peace, and they proved it by doing it.

Bibliography

Beckwith, Martha. *Hawaiian Mythology.* University Press of Hawaii, Honolulu, 1970.

Brigham, W.T. *Ancient Worship of the Hawiian Islands.* Bishop Museum manuscript, 1908.

Cartwright, Bruce. *Place Names of Moloka'i.* Bishop Museum manuscript, 1922.

Cooke, George P. *Moolelo o Moloka'i.* 1949.

Daws, Gavin. *Shoal of Time. A History of the Hawaiian Islands.* University of Hawaii, Honolulu, Hawaii, 1969.

Emerson, J.S. *The Old Gods.* Hawaiian Ethnological Notes, vol. 1, page 641, 1918.

Emerson, J.S. *Kalai Pahoa Tree of Moloka'i.* Hawaiian Ethnological Notes, vol. 2, pgs. 111-113, Bishop Museum manuscript, 1918.

Forbes, Rev. A.O. *Ai Kanaka, a Legend of Moloka'i* in Thrum's Hawaiian Folk Tales, 1907.

Fornander, Abraham. *An Account of the Polynesian Race, Its Origins and Migrations.* vol. 2, 1880.

Fornander, Abraham. *Hawaiian Antiquities and Folk-Lore.* Memoirs, vol. 4, 1916.

Grant Book. Vol. 10, Microfilm box 3, Hawaii State Land Office, Honolulu, Hawaii, January 29, 1865.

Hawaiian Government Survey. W.D. Alexander, Surveyor General, 1897.

Hitchcock, H.R. *"Touring Moloka'i."* Ke Kumu Hawai'i. Children's Mission Society Library manuscript, 1836.

Hyde, C.M. *"Rambling Notes on Moloka'i."* Hawaiian Gazette, September 17, 1895.

I'i, John Papa. *Fragments of Hawaiian History.* Bishop Museum Press, 1959.

Judd IV, Gerritt P. *Pule o o: The Story of Moloka'i.* 1936.

Kamakau, Samuel M. *Ruling Chiefs of Hawaii.* Kamehameha Schools, 1961.

Kamakau, Samuel M. *Ka Po'e Kahiko.* Bishop Museum Special Publication 51, 1964.

Kanepu'u, J.H. *"Traveling About on Moloka'i.* Ke Au Oko'a, September 5, 1867.

Ka Nupepa Ku'oko'a. *Answer to Lanikaula.* July 18, 1868.

Ka Nupepa Ku'oko'a. *The Spring of 'Olo'Olo, Moloka'i.* May 4, 1922.

Ka Nupepa Kuʻokoʻa. *A Tale of the Kona Side of Molokaʻi in the Days of Kamehameha the Conqueror.* Manuscript translation by E.P. Sterling, May 11, 1922.

Kaulili, Solomon K. *About the Menehune.* Bishop Museum Manuscript, vol. 1, pg. 407. Translation by Mary Pukui, (no date).

Kuapuʻu, S.K. *He Wahi Moʻolelo,* State Archives, 1861.

Land Commission Awards (LCA). Native Testimony Book 16, pg. 56, 1853.

Lonohiwa, David M. *The Legend Trees of Hawaii – Poison God of Molokaʻi.* Paradise of Pacific, 10-12, 1905.

Malo, David. *Hawaiian Antiquities.* Translated 1898 by Dr. N.B. Emerson, Bishop Museum Special Publication 2, 1951.

Mertz, Henriette. *Gods from the Far East: How the Chinese Discovered America.* Ballantine Books, New York, 1972.

Missionary Herald. *"Sandwich Islands: A Joint Letter of Missionaries on the Islands of Maui and Molokaʻi."* Dated November 29, 1831, 1832.

Monsarrat, M.D. Diary of Molokaʻi Survey. Manuscript, State Surveyor's Office, 1884.

Monsarrat, M.D. *Molokaʻi Surveys.* State Surveyor's Office, 1886.

Paheeikauai, R.K. *"News of Molokaʻi."* Ka Nupepa Kuʻokoʻa, August 7, 1875.

Prescott, William Hickman. *Conquest of Mexico.* Modern Library Edition, Random House, 1796-1859.

Reader's Digest. *"Dragon Ships Before Columbus."* Jay Stuller, June 1983.

Rice, William Hyde. *Hawaiian Legends.* Bishop Museum Bulletin 3.

Stewart, Charles Samuel. *Journal of a Resident of the Sandwich Islands in the Years 1823, 1824 and 1825.* University of Hawaii Press, 1970.

Stokes, John F.G. *Map of Molokaʻi.* Government Survey Chart #426, "Stokes' Heiau Locations," Bishop Museum manuscript.

Summers, Catherine C. *Molokaʻi: A Site Survey.* Pacific Anthropoligical records #14, Bishop Museum.

Tapes of Conversations with Native Hawaiians: H-91, H-91g, H-91k, H-92f, Bishop Museum.

Thrum, Thomas G. *Tales from the Temples.* Hawaiian Almanac, pg. 49-54, 1909.

Waiamau, J. *Ka Hoomana Kahiko (Ancient Worship).* Manuscript translation by Thrum. Ka Nupepa Kuʻokoʻa, January 19, 1865.

John Diamond Kauakokoulakuhaimoanakaimana Kapela Willis (known as "Koko"), was born August 7, 1928 in Honolulu, Hawaii to Laida Kealoha'ohana Paia Kapela and Kimo Kapela (later last name changed to Willis). He was raised by his grandmother Kaui Paia in the famous Paia compound along the Ala Wai Canal (known today as the Kapahulu Library and Ala Wai Golf Course). He was a gentle, kind and all around socialite to all he knew and all he would come to know. He loved and respected the 'aina and ocean, loved to sing Hawaiian songs and dance the hula, especially at the Outrigger Reef Hotel Jam Sessions. He had many talents both occupational and personal. He could be seen on several television commercials such as American Hawaii Cruises, Consolidated Theater Intros (those were cut short), Hawaii Five-O, and also KHON-TV documentaries such as "Hawaiian Hawaiian" with Leslie Wilcox and "Tales from the Night Rainbow" with Ray Lovell.

Koko was married 4 times, first marriage (wife's name unknown; she died in child birth), produced a daughter named Geminy who was raised by her maternal grandmother, secondly to Stella (no children), third to Anne Byrd on October 1960, their marriage produced 3 daughters: Stacie Kanani (Pahia), Erin Ka'iulani (Gorai), and Johnna Ane Kamaka'okalani (Thomas). Later he became a grandfather of 7: Marisa Anne Kehaulani'onakuahiwi (Willis-Javier), Jaclyn Shanel Kauakokoulakuhaimoanakaimana (Willis), Sabrina Necole (Thomas-Chandler), Daniel Michael Kala'e (Pahia), Jasmine Kapua'omailani Ku'upili'aloha (Willis-Yonahara), Matthew Jordan Kaleo'opiilani (Pahia) and Kevin Aweau (Gorai). And then a great grandfather of 5 (6th great grandchild due May 2010): Jacory Devon Ke'alii'okahale (Thomas-Hardeman), Sydney Alexandra HeMakanaMakamae'onalani (Willis), Bresha Janae (Thomas-Carney), Alayna Lilinoe (Javier), Jia Ku'upili'aloha'olaakea'okapuuwai Yotsuko (Willis-Yonahara). After their marriage dissolved, Koko continued to work for the City and County of Honolulu's Hawaiiana Department and a Chauffeur to numerous Hollywood entertainers and movie stars such as Flip Wilson, Jack Lord and Sonny & Cher to name a few and then onto Bishop Museum. Then in 1974, he met Polly "Pali" Jae Lee while working at the Bishop Museum. In 1978 they were married and he inherited 5 stepdaughters and their children. Koko lived a full life surrounded by many friends and family, he even did alot of traveling late in his life to the Continental United States visiting several Native American Indian Nations and Reservations; learning, teaching and discovering that the Native American Indians and the Hawaiians have alot in common. August 7, 1994, he celebrated what was to become his last birthday. Then on August 24, 1994, Koko who was surrounded by his loving family said his Aloha and peacefully left this earthly place to be with his Ohana on the other side of the Night Rainbow.